KINGS OF THE BLOCK 2:

THE WILLIAMS BROTHERS

DWAN WILLIAMS

GOOD 2 GO PUBLISHING

KINGS OF THE BLOCK 2: THE WILLIAMS BROTHERS

Written by Dwan Williams

Cover Design: Davida Baldwin – Odd Ball Designs

Typesetter: Mychea

ISBN: 9781947340367

Copyright © 2019 Good2Go Publishing

Published 2019 by Good2Go Publishing

7311 W. Glass Lane • Laveen, AZ 85339

www.good2gopublishing.com

https://twitter.com/good2gobooks

G2G@good2gopublishing.com

www.facebook.com/good2gopublishing

www.instagram.com/good2gopublishing

KINGS OF THE BLOCK 2:

THE WILLIAMS BROTHERS

This book is dedicated to my great grandmother (R.I.P.) Georgiana Williams-Barnes, G-Babies Jah-Ceon Moore, Alayah Neely, and Amir Neely. Also, to my family and everyone that has supported me and read my work! GOD Bless you all!!!!

Acknowledgments

I would like to thank a very good friend of mine, Harold Hall Jr., for the endless days and night helping me with the project. Words can't begin to express how grateful I am to have you as a real friend. A special thanks goes out to Kimberly and Danshauna Floyd for all of the love and support they have shown/given me throughout the years.

I would also like to thank Philip Witherspoon, Mike Wells, my cousins Erica Williams and Torey Barnes for holding me down throughout the years and my niece Arnessia Williams.

I would like to acknowledge mt people on lock that have shown their support. I will only name a few because if I name you all, this would end up a book in itself. Watkita "The Prince" Valenzuela, Jerry Partee, Frog, Fred Cloud, Hasan "Jersey" Williams, Vegas, Charles Rice, Dashuan "K-Yown" King, Rico "Polo" Moses, Demarcus "Nelly" Baxter, Michael Lawrence, Mike & Johan farmer and my entire Wide-A-Wake family.

Last but not least, I would like to acknow-ledge G2G for giving me this platform to showcase my work od art.

1

LOVE GAMES

A few months had passed since Mark and Tosha last had their conversation, and he still hadn't heard from her. He was beginning to think that he had been wrong after his conversation with Killa Mike and she really was through with him for good. He had even called a few times then hung up, just to hear her sweet voice on the other end.

The summer came and went, and it was

about time for them to go back to school. The

reality of Tosha not coming back had finally set

in, and he knew he had to move on. He knew

that giving up hustling was out of the question

just as well as he knew that having her in his life

at that time was out. He told her that after he

finished school he would give it all up and then

they could be together. He just hoped it wouldn't

be too late.

It was a Saturday afternoon and the sun was

just beginning to go down when Alex walked in

their room. "Get up, Bruh!" he shouted as he

flopped at the foot of the bed next to Mark. "I

know you ain't still fucked up over shorty, are

you?" Mark didn't want to admit it to him, but he was, so he didn't say anything at all. "Come on, Bruh, let me treat you to dinner to get your mind off of her. That should get you out of the little funk you've been in." Mark still didn't move or say anything. He really didn't want to be bothered at the time. He just continued looking at the ceiling. "We can go to your favorite spot," Alex bribed, knowing that'd change his mood. Mark looked at his brother and then shook his head as he decided to take Alex up on his offer, seeing that he wasn't going to take no for an answer. Alex smiled as he walked out of the room giving Mark some time to get dressed.

After a quick shower Mark was dressed and headed to the living room where he heard his brother talking to someone. When he entered he saw Alex, Alex's girl, Torya, and a girl he'd never seen before all sitting on the couch. "Karen, this is Mark. Mark, this is my cousin Karen." Torya pointed to one then to the other.

Karen was a true looker, and she was as close to a dime as he'd ever seen. Her clothes were top of the line, and they showed off her every curve. She wore a pair of fitted denim Levi jeans with the coat to match. Her neatly designed highlighted corn rows complimented her light brown eyes and smooth bronze skin.

Karen stood up as Mark walked over to her and then extended her hand to him. "Nice to finally meet you, Mark. I've heard so much about you."

"I wish I could say the same," Mark replied as he cut his eyes at Alex. Alex shrugged his shoulders and then tilted his head toward Torya. Mark smiled and shook his head knowing Torya was up to her old tricks of trying to play matchmaker. "Not bad," Mark thought to himself as he looked Karen over again and then let her hand loose. He could tell by the way she was carrying herself that she was not the stuck-up type that most would've thought she would be.

Torya spoke up as she saw the sparks between the two.

"So y'all ready to go? I'm hungry." Torya didn't wait for them to respond and headed for the door. Karen smiled and shook her head at how much of a hoodrat her favorite cousin could be at times. Alex was right behind her smiling as he watched her ass wiggle.

"After you," Mark politely gestured toward the door for Karen to lead the way out. "Uhm, uhm, uhm," was all he could say once he peeped her from the back. He smiled as he thought about what the night may lead to.

When Mark got out to his car, Torya was

already in the back seat while Karen waited at the front passenger's door for Mark to open it for her. After helping her in, he headed to the driver's side where Alex was standing, waiting to plead his case. "Bruh, I had nothing to do wit dis. I had no idea Torya was coming over, let alone bringing her cousin wit her." Mark gave Alex a look that let him know he didn't believe him. "She came over, I told her we were about to go get a bite to eat, and then she invited herself along with her cousin. You know how she do." Mark just shook his head, opened the door, and lifted the seat for Alex to get in. "I owe you one," Alex told his brother as he slid in the back seat next to Torya. Mark gave his brother the benefit of the doubt and told him not to sweat it. He got in, started the car, and headed to dinner.

Dinner went better than Mark had expected. He even learned that Karen was in her freshman year at AT&T University in Greensboro. After they ate, Alex paid the bill as promised. Mark then headed to Triangle Mall in Raleigh to do a little flossing. He spent thousands on a new Cuban link chain to replace the one he gave Tosha and then hit all the major designer and shoe stores. He offered to pay for the purchases Karen had picked out, and she quickly declined

KINGS OF THE BLOCK 2

the offer, but Mark paid for them anyway.

When they got back to the apartment, they all kicked it for a while before the girls called it a night. Before Karen left, she and Mark exchanged numbers and promised to stay in touch.

For the brothers the night had just begun as Alex talked Mark into going to the Crush. When they were all dressed and jeweled up they made their way out the door.

The club seemed more packed than ever as they pulled in front of the building. They received quite a few stares, even a few mean mugs, but not like they did the first time they went with Ty in his Benz. There was one thing that did stay the same: the VIP treatment the bouncer still gave them. They were about to head to the end of the line when Shy (one of the bouncers Mark delivered dope to for Ty) noticed them and waved them to the front. Mark and Alex approached Shy and gave him a pound and slid him a couple of bills as Ty did. With that they were led in without being searched. Alex wished he would've brought his strap in with him at that time.

Once in the club, they headed straight to the bar to order a bottle since they already had eaten. They ordered the same bottles as before, and when the bartender returned, Alex's eyes widened when she gave them the price. Luckily for Alex, Mark brought some extra money with him to pay for the tab. They walked to the dance floor and stood in the same spot as before and began to get their groove on. The more they drank, the more attention they received. Mark didn't know if it was the bottles or not, but he started to really feel himself.

An hour later Mark looked across the dance floor and saw a familiar face. He blinked twice to make sure his eyes weren't playing tricks on him. Tosha was surrounded by her girls sipping on a drink through a straw as she rocked to the beat. He smiled as he observed her turn several guys down that whispered in her ear. "Yo, ain't that shorty over there that we took out to eat the last time we were here?" Alex asked referring to Tosha's friend.

"Yeah, that's her," Mark responded, never taking his eyes off of Tosha.

"I'll be back." Alex made his way over to Tosha's friend and whispered in her ear. A smile appeared on her face as he led her to the middle of the floor. Tosha looked over in Mark's direction as a guy walked up behind her. She broke their stare and walked to the dance floor with the guy in tow and began to get her freak on. The more Mark watched, the more heated he became, but he remained calm not wanting to let her know that her actions were really getting to him.

"Two can play that game," Mark said to himself as a short, thick redbone turned her back to him and started winding her ass into his midsection. He could feel Tosha's eyes on him as Red Bone went to work shaking every part of her body that would shake. When he looked up he saw Tosha throw her left leg around the guy's waist and rotate her hips against him. To her surprise Mark wasn't fazed, but the guy, on the other hand, grabbed her ass and gave her a firm squeeze. She began to try to get free, but the guy wasn't trying to let her go.

"Excuse me." Mark left Red Bone where she was standing and made his way over to where Tosha was. "That's enough, playboy," Mark said as he grabbed her by her arm and pulled her away.

"Who you supposed to be?" The guy's question made Mark stop in his tracks. "This nigga trying to be Captain-Save-a-Ho," he joked. Mark had enough as he turned around and headed toward the guy.

"What you just say?" Before the guy could respond, Mark was all up in his face. A small crowd of spectators surrounded them as they anticipated a fight breaking out.

"You heard me. Did I st-st-st-stutter, muthafucka?" Mark knew by the way the guy was talking that he had no idea of who he was, but that was about to change. Just as Mark drew back the bottle in his hand, the guy was caught by a left hook that sent him stumbling backward. When Mark saw Romeo rubbing his knuckles, he smiled. By the time the guy got himself together and was about to charge at Romeo, he was airlifted into the air and slammed on his head by Alex, knocking him out cold. Alex was about to rain a few blows down on the guy until

Mark looked over the crowd and saw the bouncers headed in their direction. "Come on. Let's go," Mark told Alex and Romeo as he grabbed Tosha by her hand and escorted her to the club exit. When they got outside, Romeo saluted his cousins and jetted through the dark alley into the night. He knew Alex was a few steps behind him watching his back, so he didn't worry about anyone else trying to beef.

Alex was all hyped up as they loaded up in Mark's car. "You see how Lex put dat nigga on his head?" Alex bragged as he leaned up from the back seat.

Mark and Tosha said nothing. Mark was

about to leave. "Hold up," Alex screamed as he

looked out the window and saw the chick he was

dancing with earlier who promised him a night

he wouldn't forget if he left the club with her. "I'll

holla at y'all later."

"You straight?" Mark asked as he opened

the door to let Alex out the back seat.

"Ain't I always?" Alex responded while

patting his waistline. The ride to Tosha's house

seemed longer this time as they rode in

complete silence. Both were being stubborn and

didn't want to give in to the other. When Mark

pulled up to the curb he killed his headlights and

looked over at her. "Tosha, we need to have a

serious talk." She turned her body toward him with her arms across her chest.

"Well talk then." She rolled her eyes and then waited to see what he had to say. When Mark looked into her eyes, all the anger he had from earlier slowly started to fade away. He couldn't figure out what it was about her, but he couldn't stay mad with her for long. He shook his head and took in a deep breath before telling her what was on his mind.

"Look, Tosha, you know I care a lot about you. The feelings I have built up for you over the past year are hard for me to explain." Tosha's attitude softened the more he spoke. She knew how he felt, but hearing it come out of his mouth made a big difference to her. "I've never felt this way about anyone in my entire life," he confessed. He grabbed both of her hands and put them in his. "I never realized how strong my feelings were until I saw that guy feeling all on you tonight and I just snapped." She tried to explain that she just did that to make him jealous, but he put a finger up to her lips, so he could finish without being interrupted. "It was then when I knew that I was in love with you and would do anything for you." Tosha silently began to cry as she touched the side of Mark's face and then placed her lips against his.

When she pulled away, Mark's eyes were still closed and stayed that way for a few seconds until he heard her speak. "I'm in love with you too." They both stared at each other wondering where they were going to go from there. "Mark, I don't know why my brother trippin'. He never forbid me to see anyone before." Mark thought about lying, but he knew he could no longer keep his secret from her.

"I can't, no, I won't. She deserves to know," he pleaded with himself. "Fuck it." He gave in to his heart and came clean. "Tosha, your brother don't want you around me because of what I do, because of who I am." Tosha didn't understand what he was saying. She didn't care that he delivered groceries. She loved him for him. She was about to tell him just that when Mark continued. "Tosha, in the beginning I kind of lied to you. I lied for several reasons, and I'm sorry." Tosha sat there quietly and listened. "I lied to you because I wanted to fit into your perfect little world, so you would be proud of me, proud to be with me. I lied because I wanted to be able to provide for your every need." Her eyes began to water. "Tosha, I don't deliver groceries, I deliver drugs."

"Marquis," she called him by his real name, "I liked you for you, not your clothes, your car, your money, or your jewels. I liked you before you had any of those materialistic things, remember?" Mark thought back to when they first met, and knew she was telling the truth. "But my brother is right. We can't be together while you're still in the streets. I've seen firsthand how cold the streets can be. They don't give a damn about you nor me. Mark, I lost my father to the streets. I pray every night that I don't lose my brother to the streets as well. I can't add on one more to that list." Mark understood because he had also lost his father to the streets and wouldn't know what to do if he lost his only brother since he was the one that brought him into the game.

"Tosha, can I share something with you?"

"Anything," she answered honestly.

10 Years Earlier...

Donald and Marquis were on their way home from a long day of Christmas shopping. They sang with the carols coming from the truck's old raggedy speakers as they rode along.

Donald was a very smart and hardworking family man. He would work long days as well as nights and occasionally weekends. Lucky for him he had the upcoming holiday off, and he intended to enjoy each and every moment he had with his family over the holidays. He did everything for his woman Carolyn, their two sons, Marquis and Alexander, and their daughter, Nicole. He wasn't rich by any means, but he made ends meet and they could afford their home in the suburban neighborhood, far away from the hustle and bustle of the hood they once lived in.

When Donald pulled up in their driveway, he could hear Alexander and Nicole cheerfully playing in the living room. "Come on, son," Donald instructed Marquis as Marquis tip-toed out of the truck. Marquis did as he was told and hurriedly grabbed as many bags as he could in his small arms and then raced to the backyard to put them in the barn. On his second trip back to the truck, Marquis passed his father pushing Alexander's bike to the back. He smiled as he thought about the look that was sure to be on his brother's face in the morning when he saw it under the Christmas tree.

As Donald returned to the truck to help Marquis with the rest of the gifts, he tried not to panic when he saw the fear in his son's eyes. Before him stood two masked men. The short, stocky one of the two stood behind Marquis with one arm wrapped around his neck while he held a gun to his temple in the other one. "You know what time it is, my man, the taller of the two announced in a low but threatening tone as he scratched his arms and neck, indicating a junkie's itch.

"You can have anything you want, just don't hurt my son," Donald pleaded. "Here, you can have the money." Donald reached in his back pocket, pulled out his billfold, and tossed it over to the taller robber willingly.

"What else you got, nigga?" he greedily asked as he removed several bills from the billfold before throwing it to the ground. Donald slowly reached into the inside pocket of his coat and pulled out a small velvet box and handed it over as well. The tall robber smiled as the diamond ring inside the box sparkled from the porch light reflection. After placing it in his pocket along with the money, he went into the backyard. A minute later he returned with Alexander's brand-new bike. "You mind if I borrow this?" the tall robber asked sarcastically. Him and his partner both burst out into laughter at the same time as Donald stood there in a daze. He was too busy to hear anything they said. His focus was on trying to figure out the voice of the taller robber and where he knew him from. "Get on your fuckin' knees, nigga," the taller robber demanded, sensing Donald was about to do something foolish. After Donald did as he was told, the short robber let Marquis loose, but not before knocking him to the ground. Filled with rage, Donald jumped to his feet, but the impact from the butt of the gun quickly knocked him back to his knees.

"Come on, let's get out of here Bob before this nigga makes us kill 'em," the short one demanded before things got any uglier than they already had. It was at that very moment Donald realized who the tall robber was. His name was Bobby.

Bobby and Donald used to be old friends from the hood. They used to run together back in the day before Donald took Carolyn from him, got her pregnant, and moved her to the suburbs. That wasn't hard to do since Bobby had a small coke habit that eventually turned into a big crack habit. Bobby hadn't been the same ever since. He made a vow to himself that he would repay Donald for what he'd done to him at any cost, and that's exactly what he was doing.

"Fool, you done said my name," Bobby barked at his partner. The short robber then looked at Donald, and he immediately saw the expression on his face change from scared to angry. Donald never thought in a million years that Bobby would pull a stunt like the one he was pulling now. All that flashed through Donald's head was how he was going to seek revenge for Bobby's betrayal, and Bobby knew it. "Give me the gun," Bob demanded. Donald knew exactly what Bobby was intending to do with the gun, so he told Marquis to go into the house. He didn't want him to witness what was about to happen. Marquis got up with tears in his eyes, sensing the worse. Just as he was about to open the front door, he heard a thunderous blast come from behind him. When Marquis turned around, he saw his father lying in a puddle of his own blood, breathing heavily as the two robbers bent the corner on Alexander's bike. Marquis swiftly ran to Donald's side.

"Dad!" he screamed before kneeling down.

Carolyn came to the door to see what all the commotion was about. As soon as she saw Donald and Marquis on the ground together, she screamed at the top of her lungs. She had no idea which one of them had been shot, and it really didn't matter because she loved them both the same. As she neared, she realized that it was Donald that had been shot and instructed Marquis to go inside to call the police. Carolyn cradled Donald's head on her lap and ran her fingers through his hair to comfort him.

"I love you, Carolyn," he told her as tears trailed down his cheeks. He wasn't crying tears from the pain he was enduring; he was crying tears because he knew there was nothing he could do to stop death from taking him away from the only woman that he had ever truly loved in his life.

"I love you too, baby, now save your strength. The ambulance is on the way." Carolyn rocked him back and forth in her arms. She heard sirens nearing in the distance as she whispered about all of the good times they shared together in hopes of keeping him fighting for his life. "You're going to be alright," she promised as she wiped the tears from his eyes. She knew her last statement wasn't true when he slowly closed his eyelids followed by his bowels being released.

"Mark, I'm so sorry," Tosha said apologetically. She was fighting with herself, trying to be strong for him.

~ ~ ~

"Tosha, it wasn't your fault, and it would be selfish of me to ask you to put your life on hold for me," Mark began as he watched several tears fall down her face. "I promise you that as soon as we graduate high school, I will get out of the game and move us far away, and that's my word!"

When Mark got home, Tosha stayed on his

mind most of the night as he thought about the

events that had occurred earlier. "It'll all be over

soon," he said out loud. Then he closed his eyes

and drifted off to sleep.

2

2 YEARS LATER

So much had changed for the Williams Brothers in the last couple of years. It was now going on four years since they stepped into the drug game, and it had been nothing but good to them, but you know what they say, all good things eventually come to an end, and their thing was no different.

"Yo, Mark, let's go to A&T Homecoming," Alex said after he had finished bagging up the last two kilos of crack into ounces, halves, and quarters. Mark was tired from breaking down the previous kilo of powder into sixteenths, fifties, and dimes. Going to homecoming really hadn't crossed his mind. He really wanted to hit the block and build his bank up even more than it already was instead of taking a break to Greensboro to chase a few chicken heads. "Come on, Bruh, we deserve to have a little fun sometimes," Alex pouted after seeing Mark really wasn't interested. "What's the use of making all this money if we don't even make time to spend none of it?" Mark looked over at his brother and knew he had a point. The wheels in his head were turning. To add the icing on the cake, Alex knew what he had to say to make it a done deal. "You know you want to go and spend a little time with Karen and show off your new whip." Mark smiled as he thought about Torya's cousin Karen and how good her pussy was, not to mention her head game was on point. Every time she would come visit her family, he made it his business to dig her back out.

"That would be a good surprise, wouldn't it?" Mark thought to himself as he rubbed his chin. He also knew Alex wanted to show off his new whip as well, so he agreed. "I'll be ready in about an hour." They both stashed their dope and then took a shower before getting dressed. An hour later they were on Highway 264 headed west with Mark in his new droptop M3 and Alex following close behind in his midnight-blue GS 300 Lex.

~ ~ ~

Two hours later they were pulling up to the Four Seasons Mall. As soon as they walked in, they booked two fly-ass chicks from the ATL. "I can get used to this," Alex said after storing the number in his phone and watching the young stallion walk off. Greensboro was much bigger than Wilson, so everything about it seemed to amuse them. They walked around and did a little shopping and a lot more getting to know the chicks. Afterward they headed down the street to the coliseum to see the concert.

When they pulled into the huge parking lot, it felt more like a fashion show than anything else. The group Black Moon was the last to perform for the night, and they did their thang. All the hoodrats and dope boys were going crazy when they played "Who Got the Props." Right after that was Mark and Alex's cue to make their way out to beat the crowd that they knew was sure to follow.

In the parking lot they saw cars that they

didn't see earlier, from Bentleys and Porsches, to Double Rs and even a couple of Lambos. There were more tricked-out hoopties on chrome, such as old-school Impalas, Donks, Caprice Classics, and Monte Carlos. Those were more of Alex's kind of cars.

Mark pulled out his cell and scrolled down until he reached the *K*'s. "Bingo," he called out and then hit the connect button.

"Hello," a soft voice came from the other end. He guessed it was her roommate.

"Hi, may I speak with Karen?"

"Hold on please," the roommate said. Mark wondered what she looked like because if she

KINGS OF THE BLOCK 2

was ugly with that sexy voice, he knew she had

a lot of guys fooled. "Karen, pick up the other

phone."

"Who is it?" Mark heard her ask in the

background.

"Hold on." A second later she introduced

herself, "I'm Karen's roommate Niecy," and

asked who was calling.

"Well, Niecy, tell your friend that it's her

friend from Wilson." Niecy giggled then put the

phone down and relayed the message. Mark

heard the other phone being picked up followed

by some scrambling before Karen answered.

"Hello."

He could tell she ran to pick up the other phone by how out of breath she sounded.

"If you were busy I could call back," Mark joked just to hear her panic. He knew how much she always wanted to talk whenever he called, and when she came back at him he knew he was right.

"Never too busy for you," she replied with a big smile on her face. "I was just in the kitchen fixing me and Niecy something to eat, that's all." Mark loved how she always explained so he never had to wonder what she was doing.

"How your roommate look?" He asked wanting to hook Alex up with her, so he wouldn't be in Greensboro running the streets and possibly get in any trouble. He was also curious to know for himself as well.

"She's cool." She didn't want to say too much since Niecy had run to the doorway of the kitchen to be nosey. Niecy knew who her friend from Wilson was because every time Karen returned back to Greensboro, she would have a hundred stories about Mark and just as many gifts. She also had mentioned he had a cute younger brother. Niecy hoped she could hook up with Alex and that maybe he was generous like Mark. She told Mark to hold on for a second, and when she came back to the phone she told

Mark it would be cool for Alex to come over and chill with Niecy.

Twenty minutes later Karen was opening the door to give Mark a big hug followed by a long kiss. "I can't believe you're really here."

"Where's mine?" Alex joked as he walked by them and went into the kitchen to fix himself a drink, making himself at home. Alex looked around and asked, "Where's your roommate?" Before she could answer he walked into the living room and turned on the TV.

"She went to the store. She'll be back in a little bit," Karen responded as she grabbed Mark's hand and led him to her bedroom ready to handle their business. That's what Mark loved about her: she never hesitated when it came down to pleasing him. That's why he had no problem spoiling her.

"Niecy better not be ugly neither," Alex shouted down the hall before he heard the door slam behind them.

As soon as the door closed she was all over him. With her tongue in his mouth, she still managed to say, "Damn, I miss you so much."

"Really?" he replied between breaths. "You know I was always told that actions speak louder than words." Without saying another word Karen stepped back, lifted her Baby Phat halter top over her head revealing her firm C-cup breasts, and slid out of her booty shorts. Mark's mouth began to water just thinking about taking one of her erect nipples into his mouth. She reached down and felt his erection through his pants. "I see that someone feels my actions." She sat down at the foot of her bed then seductively waved Mark over. Mark did as she requested. She took his dick out of his jogging pants and inserted it slowly into her mouth.

"Damn," he called out. Then he put one hand on the back of her head and began to rotate his hips in a slow and steady motion. He looked down and traced the outline of her lips as she made him appear then disappear in her mouth like she was performing her own magic show. When he felt himself about to cum, he stepped back and took himself out of her mouth. She looked up at him and smiled.

"Dat ass can't take it, can you?" She knew she had some bomb-ass head, and he'd just confirmed it for her. When he sat on the bed beside her she rose up and slowly straddled him. "Ummm," she moaned out and bit down on her bottom lip in pleasure. She rocked back and forth then round and round while digging her nails into his chest, trying to control the feeling that she described as "hurting so good." She threw her head back and began to buck wildly once she got her rhythm. A true cowgirl didn't have nothing on her.

When she was done she rolled over onto her back. Mark wasn't finished with her though, so he slid back in her and then sucked on her neck and long-dicked her slowly. She wrapped her legs around his waist while stroking his back, gently soothing him while he made love to her. When he felt himself about to cum, he lifted her legs over his shoulders and started pumping in and out of her with short and forceful jabs. "Ooh, Mark, it feels so good," she cried out, feeling like he was coming through her chest. "Don't st-st-

st-stop," she stuttered then came again. When Mark came he pulled out and exploded on her stomach and breasts and then rolled over and lay on his back. The ceiling fan was full blast, but both of their bodies were covered with sweat. Karen slowly got up and walked to the bathroom to take a shower. Mark couldn't take his eyes away from the gap between her legs. He got right back hard, and before she knew it he was joining her in the shower for another round.

When they were finished and dressed they walked into the living room to see if Alex and Niecy were getting along. Karen shook her head from side to side when she saw Niecy's head bobbing up and down on Alex's lap. He lifted up a finger and put it to his lips and then put it in the air signaling for them to give him a few more minutes so he could get his nut off. They went back into Karen's room. Not wanting to be outdone, Karen got on her knees and did the same thing until Mark released another load down her throat.

This time when they entered the living room they made sure to make a little noise, so Niecy wouldn't be caught in the act again. "You ready to bounce, lil Bruh?" Mark asked. Alex sat with a big smile plastered on his face.

"I'm ready when you are." They all walked to the door, and the brothers promised they'd come back soon, before they made their exit.

On the way back, home Mark and Alex chatted on their cells to each other about going back to visit them. As soon as they made it back home, they were so exhausted that they couldn't even make it to their room. Alex flopped right on the living room couch and was out as soon as his head hit the armrest. Mark went to the recliner across from him and was about to do the same, until his cell started to ring. "Hello," he answered, wondering who could be calling so late.

"Hey, you," Karen responded. "I was just making sure y'all made it home safely."

"Yeah, we just got in," He looked over at Alex, who was now snoring. "I don't know what your girl did to my brother, but his ass is out like a light." They both laughed, called it a night, and then hung up.

~ ~ ~

It was two in the morning and Nicole had snuck out of the house again to see Rodney. He was on the way to take her back. "Oh my GOD," she gasped when he turned on her block and saw Mark's car parked in front of their apartment building. She thought that her brothers would be gone for the entire night, but she was wrong.

"What am I gonna do?" she asked in a panic.

"What's wrong?" Rodney questioned, concerned. Being that he had never seen Mark's car, he had no idea what had Nicole so uptight.

"My brothers are home!" she pointed to the black-on-black sports car parked in front of their building. Impressed, Rodney nodded his head up and down in approval.

"I see your brothers have come up since the last time I saw them," Rodney commented, remembering how raggedy they looked a while back. "I'll drop you off on the next street back, so you can sneak back in." Rodney bent the corner as Nicole thought of how considerate he was. She felt so lucky to have a guy like him in her life. Not only was he smart, but he was also fine. The fact that he always had her best interest at heart said a lot. "I'm going to circle the block a couple of times to make sure that you get into the apartment safely, so when you get to your room, turn on your television so I will know that everything is cool with you."

"Okay," Nicole agreed and then leaned over the armrest and gave Rodney a long and passionate kiss. Being that she snuck out of the apartment in her nightgown, it made it easy for him to play in her goodies for a quick second. "I got to go, baby," Nicole whispered then opened the door and slid out backward. She hated to go, but she knew if she stayed, she might give in and have sex with him. Rodney watched as she speed-walked through the alley and up the steps that led to her back door. Once she was inside, Rodney pulled off and began to circle the block like he promised.

As soon as Nicole walked in the back door, she went straight to the fridge. Her throat was parched, and she wanted a nice tall glass of apple juice to quench her thirst. "NICOOOOLE!" Mark yelled from the living room before she could take her first sip, almost making her drop the drink from her hand. Her heart skipped a beat at the thought of getting caught up in her act.

"Yes," she managed to answer calmly, not to give herself away.

"Will you bring me a glass of Kool-Aid?" he asked. Being that Mark was being so polite and actually asking for her to do something for him instead of demanding it, she was confident that her cover had not been blown. At least not yet.

"Here you go," Nicole spoke in her best "sleepy voice," acting as if she had just come down from her room to get something to drink herself.

"Thanks." Mark took the glass of Kool-Aid and downed the entire thing in three gulps. Nicole looked over on the couch and spotted Alex fast asleep with his mouth wide open. A light giggle escaped her lips, thinking about a roach crawling into it.

"Goodnight, Mark." Nicole turned on her heels and headed to the door.

"Oh yeah." Nicole stopped in her tracks at the sound of Mark's voice. "Don't be going up in my room when I ain't here spraying my cologne neither," he accused, smelling the scent on Nicole's clothes. Nicole was at a loss of words for a few seconds until it suddenly hit her what her brother was talking about.

"That's where I remembered Rodney's smell from," she thought to herself reflecting back to a few minutes prior when she kissed him good-night. It was the same fragrance that her father used to wear every time he would take their mother on a date. Just the thought of the love her parents had for each other brought a warming smile to Nicole's face. She secretly prayed that she and Rodney would share the same love one day. "Okay, daggg." She laughed and then walked out of the living room and headed to her bedroom.

When Nicole made it to her room, she shut the door and locked it and then turned on the television just like Rodney had told her to do. By the time she made it over to the window and looked out, Rodney was passing by, blowing his horn. After waving and blowing him a kiss, Nicole walked to her bed and climbed under the covers, hopefully to dream about her and Rodney's future together.

"Who the fuck is in front of the apartment blowing their fuckin' horn at this time of the morning?" Mark questioned as he pulled his gun from his waistline and walked over to the living room window to look out. When he peeked through the blinds, the only thing he saw was a glimpse of a Cadillac bending the corner down the block. Wrinkles creased his forehead as he tried to remember where he had finally remembered who owned the vehicle. Mark walked back over to the recliner he was laid back in and chalked it up as Rodney had to be blowing for one of his neighbors, then dozed off to sleep.

3

NOT GONNA BE ABLE TO DO IT

Over the next few months Mark and Alex kept their promises to Karen and Niecy and visited them every chance they got. It was becoming like a second home to Mark since he tried to fill that empty void of not having Tosha in his life. For Alex, it was just a spot he could go to chill and lay low or just get away from the hustle and stress of the streets, not to mention a get away from his main girl, Torya. Eight weeks ago, after he found out she was pregnant, she had been straight tripping. He was growing quite tired of her fussing and jealous ways. Even though Torya and Karen were first cousins, she vowed not to tell Torya of Alex's cheatings ways. She was just glad to have Mark coming over more, so if that meant her roommate hooking up with Alex, so be it. Besides, if she told on him, she would have to tell on herself for hooking them up, and she didn't want to feel Tory's wrath. She also knew Torya wasn't going to leave Alex, no matter what, so there was no way she was going to jeopardize her meal ticket for Torya.

After they finished watching *King of New York*, Karen headed to her bedroom. "Holla if you need me," Mark told his brother as he got up and followed suit, knowing what was waiting for him behind door number one. Alex threw up the peace sign and then nudged Niecy on her thick thighs, so he could wake her up and go to her bedroom.

As soon as Mark closed the door, he turned around and knew he was in for a long night. Karen was lying across her bed with both legs placed behind her head. That was one of the main reasons he loved going to Greensboro to chill with her. She was so flexible and willing to let him have his way with her. He slowly crept up to her bed. The sight of her swollen clit and fat pussy lips had him hypnotized. When he made it over to the bed he grinned devilishly. Karen did the same after looking down at the huge print in his pants. She licked her lips when she thought about how good it always tasted when he came in her mouth, and she was determined to make that her business before the night was over. "Come and get it, Big Daddy." She stuck two fingers in her opening and then patted her pussy twice. Mark wasted no time, and to her surprise he went headfirst into her wetness. She took in a deep breath not believing how good she was feeling, being that was the first time he'd ever gone down on her. She wanted to ask him what had gotten into him, but she didn't want to ruin the mood. He figured that he would return the favor since she always aimed to please him and did a hell of a job at it. She was loving it, but she could tell he was new at it. It didn't matter to her though because she was willing to teach him. Besides, it wasn't bad at all. "Right there, baby," she coached as she rotated her hips, getting her rhythm. She thought she would lose her mind from the sensation she was feeling when he went from her pussy to her asshole. "OH, MY GOODDD!!!" she screamed. Karen slung her head from side to side, took both of her hands, placed them on the back of his head, and mashed his face deep inside of her wetness. "AHHH, this is your pussy, Mark," she panted. Mark put both of his hands under her ass cheeks, lifted her up then insert his two thumbs. "What are you trying to do to me?" The more she screamed, the more his ego boosted. "UGHH," she cried out then came all over his lips. She began to shake uncontrollably, but Mark didn't let up. Even when she tried to push his forehead away, he kept eating. "Pleaassseee, Mark!" He looked up at her and then smiled while never taking her clit

out of his mouth. She tried to untangle her legs

from behind her head, but Mark held them there

with his hands.

"Dat ass can't take it," Mark laughed,

repeating the words she told him and laughing.

He sat up and wiped her juices from his face. He

shook his head as he watched her body jerk

every three or four seconds. After she stopped

she sat up in bed and looked at Mark with tears

in her eyes. Mark leaned up and kissed them

away one by one. She grabbed the bottom of his

shirt and lifted it over his head. She threw it to

the floor and began to run her fingers up and

down his chest and stomach. She replaced her fingers with her lips and made a circular motion around his nipple. Mark closed his eyes, enjoying the feeling she was bringing. He slid out of his pants, no longer able to take foreplay. She bent over to place him in her mouth, but he grabbed her wrist and pulled her up on top of him. She mounted him and began riding him like she was possessed by the exorcist, bringing them to an extreme orgasm. They both lay there spent until they drifted off to sleep in each other's arms.

The next morning Mark woke up and got dressed ready to head back to Wilson. When he walked into the living room, he spotted Alex asleep on the couch. "You ready to bounce, Bruh?" Mark asked as he pulled the cover back from over Alex's head.

"Yeah," was all he said then threw the covers off of his body, put on his shoes, and headed to the door. Mark wanted to ask him what was wrong, but he figured if he wanted to talk about it he would on their way home.

Just as Mark expected, Alex informed him that Niecy was tripping and he would no longer be taking the trips to Greensboro with him. "What happened?" Mark wanted to know. He really didn't like taking road trips by himself.

"Man, dat stupid bitch tried to give me an ultimatum. Can you believe dat?"

"What was it?" Mark asked, trying not to laugh at how dramatic his brother could be at times.

"The bitch had the nerve to tell me I had to choose between her or Torya. She knew what she was getting into before she let me hit!" Mark knew Niecy was really feeling Alex but didn't think that she would go as far as making him pick between the two. That also made him think about Karen and if she decided to trip. He made a mental note to check to see where her head was at later.

"So, what you tell her?"

"What you mean what I tell her?" Alex asked while changing the CD. "I told her it was fun while it lasted, and she kicked me out of her room and threw some covers down the hall." Mark tried to hold his laugh in but couldn't.

"No you didn't."

"SHHIITTT! Think I didn't," Alex answered, dead serious.

"At least she threw you some cover." Alex was glad of that since they kept it like the North Pole in their apartment.

"Man, I don't know what she was thinking, if she thought that I was going to leave Torya for her, or any other girl, for that matter. Me and Torya may fuss and fight a lot, but I know she has my back through thick or thin. She was here when we didn't have a pot to piss in nor a window to throw it out of." Mark knew where Alex's heart was. Torya was truly a ride-or-die chick no matter how jealous she may act. Alex let out a slight chuckle. "Besides, her pussy ain't better than my baby's."

"Aight, aight. You going too far," Mark shouted, taking his hands off the steering wheel to cover his ears.

When they made it back to Wilson, it was back to business as usual. Everything was going well for Mark even though he hadn't seen Tosha since he dropped her off at home after the club that night. They talked occasionally, but whenever Mark asked to see her she would always decline. He tried not to focus on her too much, but deep down inside it was killing him. He tried to keep himself busy by hustling overtime. That led him to spending money on things he normally wouldn't, but no matter what he did, his thoughts always drifted back to him and Tosha. Even though he didn't want to admit it, Mark was surely deep in love and was going to do everything in his powers to see to it that it never changed so they could be together when they graduated.

4

FROM SUGAR TO SHIT
SENIOR YEAR...

It was Mark's last year in high school, and he
intended on making good of his promise to
Tosha to quit the game, so they could be
together. As far as he knew she still felt the
same way because she stayed single
throughout her entire years in high school,
mainly because he made sure of it like he
promised.

The time was approaching fast, and Mark
knew he had to tell Karen they could no longer

see each other. He knew it was going to be hard to do because whether he wanted to admit it or not, he had started to grow some feelings for her. He already knew she had fallen in love with him because one night during one of their crazy sex-filled nights, she slipped up and told him.

"Damn, how am I gonna break it to her?" he thought to himself as he picked up his cell and looked through his contacts until he reached her name. He hesitated for a while before he gave in. "Fuck it," he said out loud then hit the Connect button and waited for her to answer.

"Hey, baby," she sang into the phone already knowing who was on the other end. She acted as if she was excited to hear from him.

"What's up wit you? You sound mighty happy today."

"I am," she confessed.

"Why? You act like you just passed a big test or something."

"I guess you can say that."

"That's what up. I guess I should be saying congratulations

to you." There was a moment of silence while Mark tried to find the right words to let Karen know they could no longer see each other. "We need to have a talk."

"I agree. I'll go first," she relayed without

letting him get a word in before she continued.

"I should be the one congratulating you. I'm pregnant. You're going to be a daddy!" Karen sat there quietly, hoping he would be as excited as she was, but his silence confirmed differently.

"Aren't you happy for us, baby?" It really didn't matter what he said or thought. She already had made up in her mind that she was going to keep it, with or without his help. She had planned this from the first time her cousin told her about him and his status. There was no way she was going to let her meal ticket get away from her, but what she heard come out of his mouth brought her to tears.

"I'll Western Union you the money for an abortion this weekend."

"What?" Karen screamed in tears. "I'm not getting no fuckin' abortion. I'm having it with or without you in our lives."

"Look, Karen. If you're claiming to be pregnant by me thinking that we're gonna be together, I'm telling you now that you can cancel that because we will never be together, so the best thing you can do is take the money and get rid of it and then lose my number." She removed the phone from her ear and stared at it like it was something foreign. She couldn't believe what he was saying to her.

"You ain't shit, nigga," she spat with much anger in her tone. "We'll see who gets the last laugh," she threatened before the line went dead. Mark hung up in her ear not feeling the idea of being threatened. He wanted to hop in his car and drive down to Greensboro and beat the baby out of her, if she was really pregnant.

Later that night Alex stormed into their room and began pacing the floor. He slammed his right fist into the palm of his left hand while mumbling some words. "Yo, what's up, Bruh?" Mark asked as he stood in front of Alex and put his hand on his chest and stopped his pacing. The first thought that ran through his head was they had to go handle some beef.

"I'ma kill dat bitch," Alex threatened with tears in his eyes.

"Who are you talking about? Talk to me, Bruh." Mark had never seen his brother react that way before.

"Dat bitch Niecy, man, she fuckin' crossed me and told Torya everything, I mean everything," Alex stressed as his eyes widened. He walked to the foot of the bed, sat down, and then buried his face into his hands and let the floodgates open. Mark felt bad and blamed himself for what was happening to his brother.

"Torya left me, Bruh. She said that she never

wanted to see me again." Mark wanted to tell him that her cousin Karen claimed to be pregnant by him and he left her alone, but instead he walked up to him and put his hand on his back to comfort him. That night was about to change their lives forever, and whoever stood in their way would feel their wrath.

5

ALL MONEY AIN'T GOOD MONEY

All that stayed on the Williams Brothers' minds was making money, money, and more money. They hustled from sun up to sun down seven days a week. They began to short stop on sales, and all the neighborhood hustlers could feel the effect of their wrath, and that was just the beginning of their reign. Mark and Alex were on some other shit, and Kessey was the first to feel it.

Mark pulled up on the block as Alex walked back to the stoop of their apartment building from making a sale. "What up, Bruh?" Mark asked as he walked up and took a seat beside him.

"Nuthin' much besides dis money," Alex replied as he put the money inside the rubber band with the rest of it, then put it in his pocket.

"Word, it's coming like dat?"

"What you expect, it's the first." Mark leaned back and rested himself on his elbows as another car pulled up in front of them. "You want this one?" Alex asked as he looked at the car full of crackheads.

"Nah, I left my shit in the car. Handle your business."

Alex jumped up and headed to serve the fiend until Lil Dee appeared out of nowhere and pulled out his bag of rocks.

"What y'all need?"

"I got two hundred," the crackhead replied with the crisp twenties in his hand. "So, what you gonna do for me?" His dried-up lips began to twitch as Lil Dee broke him off proper. "Thanks, youngin," the crackhead shouted as he bounced the crack up and down in his hands weighing it out. The other fiends in the car knew they had way more than what they paid for.

"Man, pull off before he try to take some back," the crackhead in the back seat shouted. The crackhead that bought it agreed and felt like the driver wasn't moving fast enough because he screamed, "Drive, bitch," before she hit the gas pedal and sped off down the block. Lil Dee took the money he just made and put it with the rest of the hundreds he had made from earlier that day. Before he could stuff the money in his pocket, Alex hit him with a powerful right cross in his ear. Lil Dee fell to the ground along with the money and the remainder of the rocks that he had in his bag. Alex picked up the pack and the money and put them in his pocket like nothing had just happened. Lil Dee looked up and wondered how he got on the ground, but quickly figured it out when he looked up just in time to see the fiend's car he just served bend the corner. Then he noticed Alex taking a seat on the stoop rubbing his fist in his hand.

"What, nigga?" Alex stood back up and headed in his direction. Lil Dee scrambled to his feet and began to wobble down the block. "Just what I thought, and don't bring yo spaghetti legs back around here neither, punk."

"You shouldn't have done that," Mark calmly told his brother as he took his seat back on the stoop.

"Man, fuck dat clown. Ain't no more money being made on this fuckin' block unless we making it." He continued to massage his fist. "Making our shit hot."

"You crazy, yo." They both laughed. "Ay, go look in my passenger's seat and grab dat bottle of Henny while I go in the house and get two cups of ice," Mark told Alex as he headed into the apartment.

When he came back out Alex had the bottle turned all the way up to his lips. "You couldn't wait, could you?" Mark asked as he snatched the bottle and poured himself a drink. They were on their third cup when they saw Lil Dee coming up the other end of the block with his Uncle

Kessey in front of him. Mark and Alex finished

off their cup and stood up in front of their steps.

Kessey walked up on the brothers with anger in

his eyes.

"Yo, what's good, niggas?" Kessey asked

with his hands in his hoody.

"You tell me," Mark shot back standing in

front of his brother.

"My nephew said your brother stole off on

him and took his shit!" Kessey was calm, but

they could tell he wanted to do more than talk.

Alex began to walk around his brother, but Mark

put his arm up to stop him.

"I got this, Bruh," Alex told Mark as he put his arm down and stood in Kessey's face. He also had his hand in his jacket pocket. "So what you come back around here fo, to get his shit back?" Alex knew the answer to the question, and so did the rest of them. Kessey could smell the alcohol on his breath and felt a little more confident about taking him out. All he had to figure out was a way to get the drop on Mark.

"Dat's right," Kessey stated. "Dat shit you took was mine, not his!" Kessey shouted as he pointed to Lil Dee. He placed his hand back in his hoody, this time clicking the safety off on his gun. He was growing tired of talking back and forth and was ready to let his banger start talking

for him. Right when Kessey was about to make

his move, Mark had beat him to it.

"Let me get dat up off ya, playboy," Mark

demanded as he held his MAC-11 to the side of

Kessy's head. Mark reached in his hoody and

pulled out a gray-and-black P-90 Ruger. "My

nigga Johnny Gill couldn't of said it better when

he said, 'My, my, my.'" He flipped the gun from

side to side admiring the nice craftsmanship of

the .45. "Now empty your pockets." Kessey had

no choice but to do what he was told. "Those

too." Kessey slowly took off his jewels. Lil Dee

just stood there in a puddle of his own piss afraid

to move.

"You wanna straighten this?" Alex asked Kessey as he stood there fuming.

"Y'all real big right now with those guns on y'all. If it weren't for that I would fuck y'all up."

"You hear this nigga?" he asked Mark, then pulled out the Uzi he had concealed in his jacket. Kessey then wished he hadn't said his last comment; maybe then he could've walked away with his life. He knew Alex had the heart to kill, but to Kessey's surprise Alex handed it to his brother. "Guess what?" Alex asked Kessey. "I don't have a gun now," Alex announced full of confidence. Kessey threw a quick jab that landed squarely on Alex's chin making his knees buckle. "Nicceee," Alex complimented as he rubbed the spot Kessey landed the blow.

"Get 'em, Unk," Lil Dee encouraged. He threw a jab in the air imitating his uncle.

"Yo lil ass gonna be next," Alex threatened as he caught Kessey with a jab to his right eye followed by a body blow to his kidney. He went down to one knee and tried to catch his breath. To his surprise Alex stepped back to let him get his shit together. He could've easily mashed him out, but he wanted to blow off some steam he had built up inside. They stood toe to toe and threw punch after punch until Alex threw a wild haymaker from left field that put Kessey's lights

out. Even though he was out before he hit the

ground, Alex caught him with another uppercut.

"UNNKKK," Lil Dee screamed as he ran to

his side. He tried his best to wake him up but

had no success. He just knew his uncle was

dead.

"Guess who's next?" Alex yelled out scaring

Lil Dee half to death. He quickly let his uncle's

head fall to the ground then jumped to his feet

and took off up the block leaving Kessey for

dead. Mark walked to the porch and picked up

the almost empty bottle of Henny and then

walked back over to where Kessey was still

knocked out at and poured it on his face.

"What you do dat for?" Alex complained as he took the bottle from his hand to finish it off as Kessey began to come to. Mark reached in his pocket and took out all of his jewelry and money and then made it rain on him like he was a stripper at a strip joint.

"Take dat, take dat," Alex told him in his best P. Diddy voice.

"This was business, nothing personal," Mark told him. "But the gun is mine, and if I see you or your peeps around this motherfucka again, it's gonna really be on." Mark and Alex watched as Kessey got up and staggered down the block. Mark wondered if he made a mistake by not pulling the trigger on Kessey. He looked at Alex, who was smiling from ear to ear. "It's about time to move Ma and Nicole outta the hood." He had a feeling that this wouldn't be the last time he heard from Kessey, so he wasn't taking any chances on his family getting hurt over a beef they didn't have anything to do with. Alex felt like it was a waste of money because he knew Kessey wasn't built like that, but he agreed anyway if it would make his brother feel better.

It took about two weeks for them to convince Carolyn to let them put her in another house on the outside the city limits of Wilson. They decided on a nice and quiet subdivision. Carolyn fell in love with it at first sight. "Thank y'all so much," she told them with tears in her eyes.

"For what? We returning the favor," Alex said with a smile.

"How much am I gonna have to pay a month for this place?" She wanted to know and make sure she could afford the payments just in case something happened to her sons. She thought back to when their daddy got killed and she had to move them back to the hood. She didn't want to go through that again. Mark smiled and then reached into his pocket and pulled out the deed. After promising they'd be back in time for dinner, they went back to the block.

To Mark's surprise their block that was always filled with kids playing their everyday ghetto games was completely empty. Mark slowly made his way down the block and parked in his normal spot in front of their apartment building and then killed the engine. Alex could tell that something was weighing heavy on his brother's mind as they made their way out of the car and onto the steps where they sat, but before he could speak on it, Mark got it off of his chest. "We should've murked that fool!" He got it off of his hand as the words came out.

"Man, I know you ain't trippin' on that nigga

Kessey." Alex laughed to himself. "The way he staggered off the block after that ass whipping, he won't be coming back around here."

"I hope you're right." Alex could see his brother still had doubt in his mind, but before he could assure him that everything was under control, an old Nissan Sentra pulled up.

"Hey, baby," Sherell called out to Alex. "Where you been? The block's been deserted for hours." She began to dig in her purse until she found what she was looking for.

"I had to make a run across town. You know how that is." Alex stopped when he got to the driver's side window and bent down and propped his elbows on the window seal. "This is how it's going to be from here on out, so if you see anyone else on the block, let me know." After agreeing, Sherell pulled out a fifty-dollar bill and passed it to Alex. When he handed Sherell her product her eyes lit up like a kid on Christmas. "Consider that a gift." Sherell knew that he was paying her in advance to let him know if she saw anyone on the block.

"I got you," she promised before putting her car in drive and speeding down the block, on her mission to get her blast on.

The day turned to night without a glitch, and before they knew it, they had sold out of everything they had. Even though Alex wanted to go to the stash and bring out more, Mark insisted on calling it a night by saying, "All money ain't good money." Alex wanted to protest but thought against it since his brother never steered him wrong in the past. They both hopped in the car with the thoughts of their girls, not to mention the home-cooked meal they knew would be waiting on them when they walked into the house.

~ ~ ~

"Nicole!" Carolyn shouted out from the kitchen.

"Hold on a second," she told the caller on the

other end. "Yes, ma'am!" she yelled with her

hand over the mouth of the phone.

"Come on down here for a minute. I need for

you to do something for me."

"Okay. I'll be right there," Nicole replied.

Then she put her ear back to the receiver. "My

mother wants me to come downstairs. Probably

to help her cook." There was a short pause as

Nicole listened to Rodney speak. "Whatever,

Rodney. I can too cook," she claimed. "I'ma

cook something for you one day to show you I

can cook."

"NICOLE!" Carolyn shouted again.

"I gotta go. I'll call you as soon as I get back

to my room," she assured him. Then she hung up before her mother came up to her room to see what was taking her so long.

For the past few weeks they had been talking on the regular. Sometimes three or four times a day. She really enjoyed their late-night conversations. They were mostly about what she wanted to do when she got older. Rodney, being that he had grown up faster than he should have, enjoyed her conversations just as well. She was different from the fast girls that he had dated in the past. She was honest and never asked for a handout, and the best thing of all, she was pure (a virgin).

Nicole unlocked her door, skipped down the stairs, and then made her way to the kitchen where her mother was standing over the sink, rinsing chicken drumsticks. "Yes, ma'am." Carolyn looked back over her shoulders at Nicole and smiled. She was growing up so fast and reminded Carolyn of herself when she was her age. Young, pretty, and smart. Not to mention a little on the naive side. Carolyn wished many nights that Nicole's father, Donald, could be there to see her now. He would surely be proud of her.

"I need you to go to the store for me and get some butter, Kool-Aid, and some sugar,"

Carolyn ran down on her three fingers. After wiping her hands on her apron, Carolyn walked over to the kitchen table where her pocketbook sat and pulled out a ten-dollar bill. "Here you go." Once Nicole took the money, Carolyn went back to the kitchen to finish cleaning the chicken.

"Okay, Ma." Nicole was about to ask for the change, so she could buy a pack of bubble gum, but thought against it. She knew her mother was struggling, so she didn't want to put any more strain on her financially, even if it was only a pack of gum.

~ ~ ~

Nicole ran up to her room, and the first thing

she did was call Rodney to let him know that she was about to go to the store. After assuring her that he would meet her there, Nicole ended the call and grabbed her jacket.

"That'll be $8.72, pretty little lady," the store clerk flirted with a devilish grin on his face. Nicole hated going to the small Arab corner store alone because every time she did, the owner tried to hit on her. Nicole went into her jacket pocket to pull out the money that her mother had given her to purchase the items. To say that the way that the owner was watching her made her uncomfortable was an understatement.

"I got this for the pretty lady," Rodney mocked the perverted store owner and retrieved a twenty-dollar bill from his pocket.

"Thank you," Nicole said shyly. She was so glad that Rodney had shown up when he did. She reached on top of the counter and grabbed the bag of items and then headed to the front entrance of the store, where she stood and waited for Rodney to get his change.

"Now that you know that she's with me, I'm sure you won't be trying to get at her no more, right?" The store owner looked into Rodney's cold, dark eyes and nodded his head in agreement.

"S-sure big man," he stuttered. Rodney turned to walk away and then turned to address the store owner again. "Oh, by the way. If she ever comes in here for anything, give it to her." After the owner assured Rodney that he understood the message he sent, Rodney walked over to Nicole.

"You ready to go?" he asked once they were face-to-face. Amazed at how much pull Rodney had, instead of answering, she nodded her head and looked at the floor. "You ready, beautiful?" he asked again. Then he placed his finger under her chin to lift her head up. Nicole blushed as she looked into his eyes.

"Yes, I'm ready," she answered.

"Good. Let's go." Rodney grabbed her free hand and led the way to his car.

On the ride to Nicole's apartment, she would occasionally sneak a glance over at Rodney. She had to admit, he was fine. Damn fine. That also made her wonder what it was that he had seen in her that made him want to talk to her. Before she got the chance to ask him, he answered the question for her, "Because you are different."

"And how is that?" she questioned, turning toward him in her seat to give him her undivided attention. Rodney took a deep breath, ran his hand over his face, and exhaled.

"You're smart, you know how to hold a good conversation, you listen to what I have to say, and you have goals." Rodney looked over at Nicole's smiling face. "And it doesn't hurt that you're beautiful too." Nicole blushed again. "You know what else will make you even more beautiful?"

"What?"

"This!" Rodney slid one of his chains over his head and handed it to Nicole. "Put it on." Nicole slid the chain on and held the half heart charm in her hand. When she looked up, she noticed that Rodney had the matching set around his neck. The only difference was his was much bigger. They made small talk until they made it to the corner of Nicole's block.

"You know you can't drop me off in front of my apartment, right?" Nicole looked at Rodney nervously.

"Yeah, I know," he assured her. Then he hit the automatic locks on the door to unlock them. Nicole put her hand on the handle, ready to make her exit, and then out of the blue she turned around, leaned in, and kissed Rodney on his lips. Before he could say a word, she hopped out of his car and headed up the block. She never looked back until she put one foot on the steps of her apartment. Rodney didn't pull off until she blew him a kiss and went inside.

"I got to make her mine," he said to himself and then drove up the block.

~ ~ ~

As soon as Mark and Alex stepped out of the car, they could smell the aroma of fried chicken lingering in the air. They couldn't wait to get inside the house and feed their faces. "Yo, Ma, I could smell the chicken as soon as I turned onto our street," Mark claimed, rubbing his hands together.

"For real," Alex agreed. "What else did you cook with that chicken?" Alex lifted the first lid and saw a pot filled with string beans and another with buttered corn, and he was sure that the big bowl in the middle of the table contained mashed potatoes. Just as he reached for the third pot on the stove top with the homemade gravy, Carolyn popped him in the back of his head.

"Go wash your filthy hands, boy!" She drew back to go upside his head again, but he stepped away from her and the stove with a quickness.

"Aight, Ma, chill, dag!" Alex laughed. Mark tried to compress his laughter as he walked out of the kitchen to head to the bathroom to wash his hands. Alex rubbed the back of his head and followed suit as he glanced at the chicken one last time.

~ ~ ~

"So, what did your mom end up cooking?" Rodney asked Nicole as he took the box of pizza out of the microwave. Big Kev and D.J. had ordered it earlier. Rodney looked at the soggy pizza as she ran down the list of food.

"Fried chicken, string beans, corn, mashed potatoes and gravy, and two apple pies." Rodney let out a deep breath and then threw the slice back into the box. "You want me to sneak you a plate before I put the food away tonight?"

she asked. That was like music to his ears. Not only would he get a chance to see Nicole, but he would also get a chance to do something that he hadn't been able to do in a long while, eat a home-cooked meal. He was burnt out on eating fast food every day.

"Let me know the time and place, and I will be there," he assured her with a smile on his face.

"NICOOOOOLE," Carolyn shouted from the kitchen. "TIME TO EAT!"

"Okay, Mother. I'll be there in a minute," she replied. "I will call you back when I finish eating and helping my mother with the dishes, so I can meet you with your food." After blowing each other kisses through the phone, Nicole ended their call and went into the bathroom to get herself together for dinner with her family.

"Well look who decided to join us," Alex huffed when Nicole walked into the kitchen. Carolyn wouldn't let him as much as take a drink of Kool-Aid until everyone was around the table. Their mother was very old-fashioned and always believed in blessing the food before they ate.

"Nicole, since you are the last one at the table, would you like to say the grace?"

"Yes, I would, Mother." Nicole bowed her

head and began saying grace. "God, I would like to thank you for this wonderful meal before us today. I would also like to thank you for looking over this household and for blessing us as each day passes by. Amen."

"Amen," they all said in unison. Alex was the first to grab a drumstick and shove it in his mouth.

"Boy, if you don't close your mouth and stop all that smacking, I know something," Carolyn warned. "That don't make no sense." She had to fuss at him every time they ate about his smacking at the table. "You act like you ain't got no home training."

"It's, 'You act as if you have no home training,'" Mark corrected, making everyone at the table burst out in laughter. They always had a good laugh when they all were together. That is what made them as close as they were.

"Ma, you really put your foot into this one," Mark complimented with a mouthful of mashed potatoes. Carolyn loved making sure that they all had a hearty meal in front of them every night. She had to admit, ever since Mark and Alex started helping out, the extra money they were giving her really came in handy and took a lot of weight off of her back. Before she got a chance to respond to Mark's last comment, he looked over at Nicole and noticed her new necklace. "Nice piece of jewelry. When did you get it?"

"Huh?" Nicole replied, almost choking on a spoonful of corn. She had forgotten to take it off before she came downstairs to dinner. "Oh, this." She knew she had to think fast and answer if she wanted to get anything past her brother. "I got it from all of the money I saved that you and Alex gave me," she lied. She could tell that Mark didn't buy her story, but she also knew that he wouldn't push the issue much further knowing that she knew their little secret on how they were really getting their money. Alex, on the other hand, was a different story. He wasn't as bright as Mark.

"When did you ever go anywhere to go buy a necklace?" Alex's question caught Nicole totally off guard because she had no idea how she was going to answer him. They all knew that Nicole never went anywhere without Mark or Carolyn taking her, unless it was to the store a few blocks away.

"I took her to get it," Carolyn intervened. She could tell by the look on Nicole's face that she was shocked that her mother had just lied for her. So was Mark, because he felt deep down in his heart that Carolyn didn't take her to purchase it. Carolyn could tell as of late that

Nicole was in so-called love by the way she floated around the house singing love songs all day and night. Being that Carolyn had traveled that same road a time or two in her days, she knew exactly how she felt. She just hoped that Nicole never went through the things she had to go through before she met their father. Carolyn made a mental note to have a talk with Nicole later on when they were alone to see how far gone she was.

Once they ate dinner, Mark and Alex stepped out to head to the mall to grab a few new outfits for the weekend. They planned to go to the Orange Crush again to see what they could get into, and of course to show off Mark's car. That gave Carolyn enough time to pry into her daughter's love life a little.

After Nicole told Carolyn about Rodney, at least what she knew about him through their phone conversations, Carolyn gave her blessing, with a little advice of course. "Never let anyone make you do anything that you are not ready for!" she stressed.

"Rodney's not like that, Mother," Nicole assured her. Carolyn kissed Nicole on the top of her forehead and walked out of the kitchen, with hopes that she wouldn't get hurt on the road called love.

By the time Nicole fixed Rodney's plate and checked on her mother, Carolyn was fast asleep. Even though she didn't have to work half as much, when she did, it drained her. That was cool with Nicole; that just made it much easier for her to sneak out and see Rodney. After calling him and giving him the place to meet her at, Nicole was out the door. She just hoped the decision she was making didn't come back to bite her in the butt.

~ ~ ~

Nicole had talked Carolyn into dropping her off at the movie theater, but instead of going to watch a movie with Rodney, they made other plans to go to his house and chill.

They pulled up to the front house, and like a perfect gentleman, Rodney opened her door for her and led her to the front door. When they walked inside, Nicole was amazed. It was nothing like she had thought. His place was well furnished, neat, and in place. Rodney put on *Juice* and sat on the couch next to Nicole, who cuddled comfortably in his arms. He tried to invite her to his bedroom a couple of times, but she politely refused. Rodney wasn't used to getting rejected, but he kept in mind that Nicole was young and most of all was a virgin. "So, have you told your brothers about us yet?" he questioned, never taking his eyes off of the huge floor-model television that sat in the middle of the spacious living room.

"No, not yet," Nicole replied. She then positionned herself a little closer to him. That was the same line she replied with every time he would ask her about it. Being that they had been talking for a little over a month now, Rodney's patience with the situation was growing very thin.

"Are you ashamed of me or something?" he sat up and asked, making Nicole rise up from under his arm.

"No, Rodney, you know that's not it!"

"Well what is it then?"

Nicole looked down at her hands and began to play with them. "Rodney, you just don't understand. My brothers are different when it comes to me. They are very overprotective," she tried to explain, but Rodney wasn't trying to hear it.

"So, what? You gonna let them nigga's run your life forever?"

"No, but—" Nicole began to say defensively, but Rodney cut her off.

"But what then?" Nicole had no response. "Look. Am I your man?" Nicole nodded her head up and down. "Well you need to act like it and respect our relationship. Are you gonna do that?" Again, Nicole nodded her head in agreement. "Good!" Rodney lifted Nicole's head up and stared into her eyes. "I love you, Nicole," he whispered. Then he leaned in and pressed his lips against hers. Nicole couldn't believe her ears.

"I love you too," she replied between kisses. Rodney slowly lay her down on the couch and began to run his hand up her skirt.

"Rodney!" Nicole protested with her eyes still closed. Her mind reflected back to the many nights she touched herself, wishing it was Rodney. She didn't think it was possible, but it felt even better than she imagined. Nicole lowered her hand to his midsection and felt the length of his penis. "I'm not ready," she said after feeling his erection. He was much bigger than she thought.

"Come on, baby. I'm gonna take it easy with you." Nicole felt herself getting wetter from each word that he whispered into her ear.

"I'm scared," she whispered back.

"I got you," he promised her as he slid his erection out of his jogging pants. Rodney gently slid her panties to the side and lubricated her vagina with his pre-cum.

"Ouuuch," Nicole cried out. "Stop please!"

she begged, but her cries fell on deaf ears.

"Rodney," she screamed as he went in and out of her with force, but he didn't slow up. Nicole scratched and clawed at his back until he released his load inside of her. When Rodney was finished, he put himself back inside of his jogging pants then went into the bathroom to get himself together.

When he came back out, Nicole was still lying on the couch balled up. "I love you, baby," he told her as he sat down beside her and began cleaning up the blood from between her legs. "She really was a virgin," he said to himself. After helping Nicole to her feet, they headed out the door, back to the movie theater before her mother showed up. As soon as they stepped on the front porch, the first people they saw were Big Kev and D.J. "Sounds like y'all had a good ole time in there," Big Kev laughed. He was quickly silenced by the deadly look Rodney gave him after his comment. "My bad!" A tear slowly trailed down Nicole's cheek as she walked past Big Kev and D.J. to the car.

"I'll discipline you when I get back," Rodney threatened as he walked off the porch behind Nicole.

~ ~ ~

As soon as Rodney dropped Nicole back off

at the theater, Carolyn rolled up. "Did you have fun at the movies?" she asked her daughter.

"It was alright," Nicole replied looking out the window. Her mind was in another place, and Carolyn could tell. Instead of prying, she let Nicole be. She knew that if she wanted to talk about it, she would. Until then she would let her live and learn from her own mistakes, the way she had to coming up. She just hoped that Nicole made better decisions than she did.

6

WHAT'S BEEF?

It was going on a month since Alex put the beat down on Kessey, and to their surprise it had been quiet ever since. Everyone knew whose block it was and didn't dare to come to sell any dope on it. The brothers had clearly sent the message they wanted to send to anybody that thought they could sell on their turf.

"What up, kid?" Ty asked as he pulled up to the side of Mark's car.

"Not too much." Mark reached out his window to give him a pound. Ty leaned his head to look over Mark's shoulder to acknowledge Alex sitting in the passenger's seat sipping on a bottle of Vodka.

"Can I hold something?" Ty joked.

"SHITTT! If I had yo' hands I'd cut mine off," Alex joked back.

"Yeah right, Mike Tyson," Ty said. Then he directed his attention back to Mark. He couldn't believe how determined the two brothers were. It seemed just like yesterday when they were making deliveries for him, to him frontin' them packs, to them being able to buy their own now.

They had come a long way from the bottom to damn near the top. "Ay, I got a nice deal for y'all, if y'all are interested." Alex sat up in his seat to hear what he had to say, just as Ty knew they would. He knew it was a deal they couldn't refuse.

"You know we always down for a come-up," Mark replied honestly waiting to hear what the deal was.

"Yeah, we trying to reach yo' status," Alex cut in, rubbing his hands together.

"Dat's wassup. I got four bricks of coke left and I'ma let y'all get 'em for twenty grand a piece, ONLY because I fuck wit y'all. The thing is, I need the money in the next hour because I'm about to meet wit dis new connect and I'm seventy-five grand short." Ty knew that was a lot of cash to come up with on such short notice, but he knew with the work they were copping from him that they should be able to handle it with no problem between the two. Little did he know they had that and more. As a matter of fact, as they discussed it amongst each other, they wanted to put more in with him to get an even better price. Mark told Alex that they would see how it went first and add that on the next re-up.

"We'll take 'em off your hands for you, big

homie," Mark told him.

"Good. Come by my spot in an hour," Ty informed them before pulling off down the block. Mark and Alex made their way into their apartment to get the money from out of the safe hidden in the floor.

Thirty minutes later they were on their way to Ty's spot on the west side of town. As they pulled up to the light, the brothers felt like Tupac. It was like all eyes were on them. Chicks were smiling and waving hoping they would scoop them up and take them for a ride. The guys, on the other hand, were on the sideline hating as usual.

When the light turned green Mark began to slowly pull off making sure the haters could hate a little longer. Special Ed's "I Got It Made" was blasting through the sound system, when all of a sudden things seem to move in slow motion. When Mark looked over to Alex, he saw a guy reaching in through the passenger side window with a gun in his hand. Just as he tried to warn Alex, the guy let off two shots that sounded like canon rounds. BOOM . . . BOOM . . . That was followed by a voice saying, "Who's laughing now, motherfucka?" Alex had his Uzi in his lap but was unable to grab it in time. Everything happened so fast. Alex was hit in the upper shoulder and the head. The gunman tried to let off another round to make sure he finished the job, but his gun jammed up. That gave Mark just enough time to lift his MAC-11 off his lap and let off a three-round burst: TAT, TAT, TAT. He struck the gunman all three times in the chest lifting his body in the air and then onto the ground. By that time the streets were in a frenzy. Chicken heads, kids, and hustlers all made a run for cover. By the time Mark made it through the intersection, it was all over. What seemed like five minutes only lasted about five seconds.

"Hold on Alex!" Mark yelled over the loud music. As he ran every red light in sight, he did something he hadn't done in a long time. "GOD, please do not take my brother from me. Let him make it through this and I promise I'll do whatever it is that you want me to do." When he finished, he picked up his mobile phone and called 911 so they would be prepared once they arrived at the ER entrance.

When they arrived, Alex was rushed into surgery. Mark hoped that his brother would pull through this, but he had some doubt because of all the blood he had lost on the way there. The gunshot wound to the head was what really worried him. All that went through his head was who could've done it and why. He kept replaying the day's event over and over in the back of his mind.

An hour later the entire waiting area was filled with family, friends, and spectators. Torya was taking it the hardest out of everyone there. She had passed out three times while they waited for the doctor to come from the rear with an update. Mark was trying to stay strong for her and his family, but it was slowly breaking him down. He didn't know how much longer he would be able to hold it together. "Is he going to be alright?" He heard a familiar voice ask him from behind. He turned around, and it was like he was looking in the face of a real, live angel.

He stared up at Tosha, and she could tell by the look in his eyes that he was hanging over the edge. She embraced him in her arms to absorb some of his pain.

"We don't know yet. All we can do at this point is pray for the best." It was then he let his tears flow freely.

"It's going to be okay." Tosha rubbed his back in a circular motion while gently patting it. He felt so much better in her arms. A chill ran through his body, and he looked up toward the entrance. Him and Killa Mike locked eyes before Killa Mike turned and walked out the door. Mark took a step back and looked into Tosha's teary eyes. He wondered if she knew her brother had come. He didn't want to get her in any trouble, and he definitely didn't want any beef with Killa Mike at that time.

"Do your brother know you are here?"

"Yes. He's the one that brought me here to be with you." Mark was thankful for her brother doing so because he needed her now more than ever. All sorts of thoughts began to go through Mark's head. He started to think everyone was suspect, even Killa Mike. He wondered if he was using his sister to find out if Mark or anyone else had any idea he was behind the hit. Mark's mind was going a hundred miles per hour. "Oh yeah, he wanted me to tell you that he needed to talk to you about something."

"About what?" Mark wanted to know, but before Tosha could continue, the doctor appeared from the back with Alex's update.

"How is he, Doc?" Carolyn asked meeting him halfway.

"He's going to pull through." They all breathed a sigh of relief. "He's a very strong and determined young man. We lost him twice on the table, but he fought and came back. It's like the kid got nine lives or something," Doc joked. After seeing that no one thought that was funny, he told them that they would be able to see him once he got some rest. Tosha gave Mark a big hug and a kiss. When he pulled away he noticed two police officers come in and head to the check-in desk. A couple of seconds later he saw them turn and head in his direction. He turned to Tosha and looked her in her eyes. "I need for you to do me a big favor." Before she could ask what it was, he handed her his car keys. "Look in my back seat and take the book bag out and take it to your house and put it up. I'll be over there as soon as I leave here." She was about to ask what was inside of the book bag, but before she could he kissed her on her forehead. "I'll see you in a little bit."

"Excuse me, sir. May we have a word with you please?" Tosha walked away slowly. Before she walked out the door, she took one last look back as a tear slid down her face.

"What's up?"

The officers asked him question after question. The more they asked, the more upset they became. Mark told them nothing that could help them out, not even what the guy had on. Mark had it in his young mind that he was going to get whoever tried to take him and his brother out. Besides, there was no way he was going to break the code of the streets and help the pigs out in any kind of way. After thirty more minutes of getting nowhere, they handed Mark their card and told him if he could think of anything to give them a call.

Mark took a seat in the chair across from his mother and sister as they slept. The scene of the shooting stayed in his head. For the life of him he couldn't figure out who hated him and Alex bad enough to want them dead. He had a few people in mind, but not one with enough heart to come at them, in broad daylight to make matters even worse. That meant they didn't give a fuck if anyone saw them. He thought long and hard until he dozed off into a deep sleep.

"Marquis, Marquis. Wake up!" Nicole told

him as she continuously shook him awake. Mark opened his eyes and looked at her like she was crazy. "Alex is asking for you." He wasn't sure he heard her right until she said it again.

"Alright, I'm up." He looked around the empty waiting room and asked, "Where everybody at?"

"Mama sent everybody home. She told them to come back tomorrow." Mark got up, stretched, and then followed Nicole to the elevator. When they got off, Mark received odd looks from the people around him. He figured it was because he still had on the bloodied clothes from when he brought Alex in. When he got to Alex's room he slowly opened the door. Carolyn was standing over him with his hand in hers saying a silent prayer. When he walked up to the bed, he instantly broke down at the sight of his brother. He wasn't used to seeing him looking as vulnerable as he was then. His head was wrapped up and twice its normal size. "I'll be outside," Carolyn said, no longer able to take her two boys in so much pain. Mark watched her leave and then pulled up a chair and sat at Alex's bedside. He placed his head on the bed and began to pray. When he finished he heard Alex mumble something. Mark got up and leaned in closely, so he could hear what he had said. When Alex spoke this time, Mark just smiled and shook his head.

"You wish you look better than me," Mark responded, wiping away his tears. The more he looked at his brother, the more all he could think was someone had to pay. "Bruh, when I find out who did this, they're dead." Alex closed his eyes and a single tear rolled down his cheek before he spoke.

"Let it go, Bruh." Mark thought he heard him wrong and told him to repeat himself. "You heard me right. I said let it go, for me. It's time to move on from this shit. We've made more than enough money, but what good is it if we don't even live to enjoy it?" Mark knew what his brother had just said was true, but what he asked him to do was a hard pill to swallow. Mark knew if the shoe was on the other foot Alex would go out with his gunz blazing for him, and he couldn't picture himself not doing the same. Mark figured it was just the meds talking for him. Right when Mark was about to tell him how he really felt, their mother entered the room, so they changed the subject.

"Mark, will you please go and pick up Torya? That child gonna have a fit if she don't get herself up here." Alex tried to smile, but the bandages were making it hard for him. Mark agreed to go get her. He knew that would be a good time for him to change clothes, and to put

his ears to the streets. He also needed to go pick

up the money and guns from Tosha's house.

When Mark got home the first thing he did

was call Tosha. She had been worried all night

since Mark never called or came by. He assured

her that he would be over as soon as he

dropped Torya back off at the hospital and

talked to Killa Mike. After finding out Torya had

already caught a cab to the hospital, he headed

to go see Killa Mike.

Mark hopped in Killa Mike's Escalade ready

to find out who was behind the attempt on their

lives, but the news Mike had for him felt like

somebody stabbed him in the back with a machete. "Are you sure?" Mark asked, not wanting to believe his ears.

"I'm positive, Son. He told me with his own mouth." Mark was ready to go to war at that very moment. He took a deep breath and began to put his plan together. He knew it wouldn't be easy and he couldn't make any mistakes, or he might end up like Alex—or even worse, dead!"

"I can't believe this nigga tried to murk me and Alex. He knew firsthand how we get down for ours. He gonna get his, though. I put dat on my daddy!" Mark said out loud.

"You good?" Killa Mike asked, snapping him

out of his zone.

"Yeah, I'm good. Thanks for the info, Bruh, I mean, Killa Mike." They gave each other some dap and then Mark jumped into his car and headed to Tosha's.

"You bullshittin'," was all Tosha could say after Mark ran down what Killa Mike had told him. "Mark, promise me you won't go and do nothing stupid." Without giving her a promise, he began running down his plan and what he wanted her to do with his book bag if anything happened to him. In tears, she agreed. "I love you so much, Mark," she told him as she hugged him and gave him a kiss.

"I love you more, beautiful," Mark responded, placing both of his hands on the sides of her face. He then headed for the front door to make his exit. "Good-bye, Tosha."

"Don't say that, please. Good-byes are forever. I'll see you later." He smiled and knew he loved her more than he loved himself. No matter how bad things had seemed in his life, she always knew how to brighten things up for him.

"See you later." Mark walked out the door and got in his car as Tosha went into her room and cried herself to sleep.

7

PAYBACK'S A BITCH

"I bet fifty my nephew hit the nine," Unk called out looking for a potential bet.

"Bet dat," Lamont accepted, throwing a fifty-dollar bill down in front of him. Unk threw the fifty down on his.

"Eight," Unk called out as his nephew rolled a five and a three.

"Fifty more," Lamont yelled out feeling himself. He was playing big money in front of the spectators that had started to form around them.

He spotted two hoodrats that he been wanted to

dig out, and he knew if he got lucky on the dice

he would be able to afford them.

"A hundred more if you wanna bet

something, my man. I ain't got all day to be out

here fuckin' wit you!" Unk shot back knowing

Lamont's money was nowhere near as long as

his.

"Bet dat," Lamont replied in a lower tone this

time. Lil Dee rolled about four more times before

he crapped out. "Let me get my money," Lamont

said like Smokey from the movie Friday. He bent

over and picked up all the money from the

ground as he licked his pointer finger and thumb and then slowly started flicking through the fifties and hundreds.

"Bet back. Double or nuthin," Unk challenged, pulling out more money than Lamont could've made even if he hugged the block for two weeks straight. Unk could see the wheels turning in Lamont's head, so he pressed harder. "Fuck it, triple or nothing." That had Lamont sold once he calculated the three grand he had in his hand could easily turn into nine in a minute or two.

"Only if you roll," he stipulated. Then he sat the money down up under his Timbs.

"Give me the dice, nephew." Lil Dee did just that then stepped back so Unk could do his thing. Little did Lamont know, Unk was much better of a shooter than Lil Dee ever was. Unk rolled a four on one dice and a six on the other. "Your point is then, kid!" After rolling two more times Lamont started to grow some balls once he heard two chicks in the background talking about how much they had bet.

"You gonna bet some more or what?" He was thinking about all the hundred-dollar bills Unk still had on him. Lamont was determined to leave from there with at least half of them. He already had which hotel he was gonna take the two chicks he had his eyes on earlier to. Unk rolled the dice again and then snapped his fingers.

"Get 'em, girl," he called to the dice, watching one land on five and the other spinning around until it landed on five also. "You lose, chump." Lamont's chin dropped to his chest. When he looked up, the two girls turned their attention to the money Unk was picking up off the ground.

"Nah, you lose," a hooded stranger announced as he walked through the crowd of onlookers. "UUNNNKKK," Lil Dee screamed as he tried to get his Uncle Kessey's attention before the hooded man pulled the trigger, but he was a second too late. The MAC-11 ripped through his chest and back as each bullet spun his body around. Bystanders immediately ducked and ran for cover as the fireworks erupted. When the gunfire ceased, Mark walked up to where Kessey's body lay sprawled out on the ground. He squatted down beside him as Kessey tried to catch his breath.

"So that's how you survived the first time," Mark said out loud then ripped open his shirt and revealed the bulletproof vest underneath. Kessey looked through strained eyes as Mark removed the hoody from over his head. "The vest won't save you this time. When he was finished Kessey was a bloody mess.

"Fuck you, nigga," Kessey howled out in pain.

"Nah, my nigga, fuck you."

By the look in Mark's eyes, Kessey knew his death was near, so he said what a real G would have said under the circumstance: "See you in hell, motherfucka!" Then he spit blood on his shoes. His words were followed by round after round that all found themselves a home in his head and face.

After completing what he had come there for Mark turned and headed back in the direction he came from. BOOM was all he heard as his body stiffened. He closed his eyes and prepared for the worst. When he heard a body tumble to the ground, he opened them back up and turned around and saw Kessey's nephew Lil Dee laid out in a puddle of his own blood. Lamont was running both of their pockets before he made eye contact with Mark and then made his exit through a nearby alleyway. Mark turned and did the same thing as he heard sirens nearing.

~ ~ ~

"Hi, Rodney. I was wondering if you could come by the hospital and pick me up?" Nicole asked when he answered his phone. "He going to make it . . . I'll be okay. I just need you right now . . . Okay. See you in a few." Nicole hung up the receiver of the phone booth and headed out of the lobby back to her brother's room where Carolyn sat in a chair reading her Bible. "Mother, I'm about to catch a ride home with a friend from school," Nicole whispered to Carolyn, trying not to wake Alex.

"Okay, baby," she whispered back. Nicole kissed her mother on the cheek and headed toward the door. "Oh, Nicole?" Nicole turned around with a big smile on her face.

"Yes, ma'am."

"Tell Rodney that I said hello."

"Okay," Nicole replied and then turned and

walked out the door. She swore before she did, she saw Alex frown his face up. "Maybe I'm just trippin," she summed up before heading to the front entrance.

"You look beautiful," Rodney complimented the way her skirt fit her curvy frame when she sat down in the passenger's seat.

"Thank you." She blushed and then placed her hands on her lap.

"So where to?" he asked as he pulled out of the hospital parking lot into traffic.

"Can we go to your house?" she asked. "I need you to hold me." She didn't have to ask twice because Rodney was thinking the same thing. They hadn't had sex in two weeks, and he had been dying to try his new trick on her since then.

Fifteen minutes later, they were walking down the hall to Rodney's bedroom. "We need to have a talk, Rodney." He figured that it was about time for Nicole to ask him to commit to her. He was surprised that they hadn't had that talk sooner. Rodney grabbed Nicole by her hand and led her to the foot of his bed where he sat her down.

"What you want to talk about?" Rodney asked as he stood over her and ran his fingers through her hair. Nicole closed her eyes and took in a deep breath.

"I think I'm pregnant!" She waited patiently for Rodney to respond, but he never did. When she opened her eyes and looked up, Rodney was smiling from ear to ear. "You're not mad at me?" she questioned.

"Mad at you. For what? For making me the happiest man in the world?"

"Don't get your hopes up yet. I'm just three weeks late for my cycle."

"Well make a doctor's appointment first thing Monday morning and I'll take you to see wassup." Nicole's heart melted, knowing that if she was pregnant, Rodney had her back 100 percent. She wished that her father was there to meet Rodney. She knew that Donald would love him too. Nicole opened her legs wider as Rodney slid up closer in front of her. After removing his gun from his waistline, Rodney bent down and sat it on the floor, sneaking a peek at Nicole's cherry-red panties. On his way back up, Rodney leaned in and kissed Nicole on her lips. She assisted Rodney with sliding out of his pants and then lifted her skirt over her hips. She watched Rodney lift his shirt over his head and throw it in the far corner of the room. Nicole began planting soft kisses on his stomach as he ran his hand through her hair once again.

"What are you doing, Rodney?" she asked him as he guided her head a little further down.

"Kiss it," he coached as he grabbed his shaft with his other hand.

"I've never done that before," she replied, fighting to lift her head up, but his grip was too strong.

"Just try it, damn!" he insisted.

"I don't want to!"

Rodney placed his erection on her lips and then yanked her hair, making her snap back.

"Ouchhh!" she screamed.

That was the break that Rodney was looking for.

Just as he was about to shove his penis into her

mouth, a series of gunfire erupted outside.

~ ~ ~

Mark and his cousin Romeo had been riding around for hours trying to find Ty. Romeo was known in the city for his ruthless actions when it came down to gunplay or beating a nigga down. People knew when he showed his face someone was about to pay.

They had been by each and every one of Ty's known hangouts, trap houses, and baby mama's houses, but he was nowhere to be found. Mark was becoming impatient and was about to call it a night when his cell phone began to ring. "What?" he answered in an annoyed tone. The caller had their number blocked, and he hated for people to do that.

"It's Lamont," the caller replied in a calm voice. Mark took the phone from his ear and looked at it like it had two heads.

"Lamont who?"

"You don't actually know me, but—"

Mark cut him off after he said that. "So why are you calling my phone?"

"Like I was saying, you don't know me, but I did you a favor earlier today and I'm sure the info I got for you is even bigger than that. That's if you want it." Lamont had Mark's full attention then, and he calmed down after recalling the incident from earlier.

"My bad, and I appreciate what you did for me earlier. I was just telling my peeps about dat. I owe you one, kid."

"Nah, you good, real recognize real. Besides, I got mine back and more." They shared a laugh at how Lamont ran the two corpses' bodies before Mark got back to the situation at hand.

"So what kind of info do you got for me?"

"I have one condition before I tell you." He didn't wait for Mark to agree, because he knew he would. "You gotta let me roll with you to get Ty." Mark was hesitant at first because he didn't know anything about Lamont. For all he knew it could have been a set-up. He brushed that idea out of his head remembering the look he had in his eyes after he killed Lil Dee without even a second thought. The look reminded him of the time he saw Alex kill his first prey.

"You got a deal."

Once they picked up Lamont, he ran down the information he had on Ty and his new spot. That would be the first place they looked. As they rode in silence, the same question kept going through Mark's head. "So why you got it out for Ty so bad?" For the first time Lamont broke his demeanor and focused out the window, and Mark could tell he was trying to fight back his tears.

"H-h-he killed my sister," Lamont stuttered. Mark's heart went out to the young thug as he looked at him through the rear-view. Even though he hadn't lost a sibling, Alex being in the hospital made him feel some of his pain. Now he understood the taste for revenge Lamont craved, but he still wanted to know more.

"How did he kill her?"

"He gave her AIDS," Lamont answered, and then began to tell the story.

~ ~ ~

Lamont was awakened out of his sleep in the

middle of the night by the sounds of his sister, Jocelyn, and her boyfriend, Tyrell, who she would sneak into the house every time her father worked third shift. "How could you, Ty?" she cried out. Lamont slowly made his way out of bed and into the hallway where he stood at Jocelyn's bedroom door and peeped through the crack and looked in. For the life of him, Lamont couldn't understand why his sister just didn't cut Ty off, since she was young, smart, pretty, and had the body that put women that tried to stand next to her to shame.

"Girl, you keep listening to them bitches in the street. You gonna find yourself by yourself!"

Ty threatened. Then he checked his pager for the fifth time since he had been there. He hated to be missing money, especially when Jocelyn didn't want to do anything but pick a fight with him over every little thing.

"Who is that, Tyrell? One of your little stankin'-ass bitches?" she accused, then slapped it out of his hand. Ty balled his fists and took in a deep breath, trying to control his growing temper. He knew he had to get out of there, and quick, before he did something he was sure to regret in the future.

"Yo, you trippin', Jocelyn. I'm outta here!" Ty shook his head and turned around and headed for the door. Lamont almost sprung his ankle trying to make it back to his room without being seen.

"And take this with you, you sorry-ass motherfucker!" Joselyn cursed then walked over to her dresser, picked up a foreign object, and threw it at him. Ty caught it in mid-air and looked at it.

"Positive," he said with a confused look on his face.

"Yeah, that's right, nigga. I'm pregnant!" All of the anger and frustration that Ty had at that time turned into joy and happiness at his newfound news. It was quickly replaced when the next words came out of her mouth. "I don't know why you all happy and shit, because ain't no way I'm about to bring a baby into this world with AIDS," she assured with tears in her eyes. Ty looked shocked.

"What the fuck you talkin' about, bitch?" Jocelyn looked at Ty like he had lost his mind.

"Bitch? You call me a bitch and you the one out fuckin' random broads and gave me AIDS? You got some fuckin' nerve." Ty was about to speak on her accusations, but she interrupted him. "And don't you dare come outta yo' mouth and try to blame me, because we both know that I never been with anyone else besides you," she shouted honestly, getting up in his face. "I'ma

tell everyone about yo trifflin' ass," she

promised. Before she could get any more

threats out, Ty grabbed her by the throat and

shoved her back hard into the wall.

"Bitch, if you tell anybody I gave you AIDS,

I'ma kill you ass," he promised. Then he stared

into her eyes before giving her one last

squeeze. Ty stood to his feet as Jocelyn

grabbed her neck and tried to breathe in as

much air as she possibly could. She slid down

to the floor as she watched Ty turn and walk out

of her room.

"I hate you!" she screamed as he walked

down the hallway to the front door. It wasn't until she heard Ty's car speeding off into the night that she realized Lamont had entered her room.

After confiding in her little brother, the only person she could trust with her secret, they talked, hugged, and cried together for a few hours. Once Lamont was sure that she would be okay, he went back into his room and climbed into bed. He didn't even know that he had dozed off until he heard the thunderous sound echo through the air. When he ran into his sister's room, he discovered her with the side of her head blown off and a suicide note clutched in her left hand. No sooner than he finished reading it did Jocelyn's phone began to ring.

Lamont picked it up and saw Ty's name pop up

on the display screen.

"Hello," Lamont heard the familiar voice that

he hated so much. "Hello," Ty repeated when he

got no response. "Baby, I'm sorry," he

apologized. Lamont listened on the other end of

the phone as Ty poured his heart out.

"I'ma kill you, nigga!" Lamont promised.

Then he threw the phone into the wall,

shattering it into little pieces.

Mark and Romeo were speechless and

damn near in tears by the time Lamont finished

telling the story of why he wanted Ty dead.

The rest of the ride was made in silence. They all were lost in their own thoughts until they reached their destination. "There goes the spot right there," Lamont informed as they rode past a two-story fenced-in row house. They went to the end of the block and turned around and then parked on the other side of the street. Now all they had to do was sit and wait for Ty to come collect his money.

"You sure he coming?" Mark asked. They had been sitting for an hour straight.

"I'm sure, big homie." Lamont was confident as he looked back at the spot. He hoped Mark believed him and didn't start thinking crazy like he was trying to set him up or anything like that. Little did Lamont know that was exactly what he was starting to think. Mark gave Romeo the plan of what to do if Lamont was lying before they picked him up. As Romeo pointed the gun to shoot Lamont through the seat, he yelled, "There he go right there." Romeo was glad because he really liked the kid. Ty jumped out of his S420, opened the fence, and then walked into the spot.

"Let's go," Mark ordered as soon as the door closed behind Ty. Lamont and Romeo went inside the fence and posted up on both sides of the house. Five minutes later Ty came out with a Gucci knapsack on his back with an unlit blunt dangling from the right side of his mouth. Before opening his car door, he patted his pants pocket looking for his lighter.

"Damn," he cursed himself, remembering he had let one of the niggas in the house use it. When he turned around to go back into the spot, he noticed a fiend walking by. "Yo, let me get a light from you." Ty reached in his pocket to give him $20 for his assistance.

"Always look a man in his eyes when you're talking to him." Ty looked up and saw Mark pointing his MAC-11 in his face. "He'll respect you more," Mark finished the last part to the first lesson Ty had ever taught him. "Ain't that what you've always told me, huh? Do you respect me now?" Ty didn't answer. "You look surprised. I wonder why. You always said I was the smart one, didn't you?" Ty grinned as he looked in Mark's eyes. He could see the hurt and pain in them. He never in a million years thought he would get caught slippin' like he had. Ty knew Mark wasn't a thoroughbred killer, so he figured he would try his gangsta.

"What you waiting for nigga? If you gonna shoot, SHOOT!"

Ty was getting a little loud trying to shake him up, but more than anything he wanted to get the attention of the young gunners in the spot.

"Just like I thought, without your brother, nigga, you ain't shit." The words cut Mark like a double-edged sword. He never thought he would be betrayed by the one person he looked up to most in his life.

"I just got one question for you before I send you where I sent your flunky-ass homeboy." After hearing those words, he began to regret what he had just said. He heard Kessey got killed during a dice game, but Mark never crossed his mind as being the killer. He looked in Mark's eyes again, and it was then he noticed his life would soon be coming to an end. "Why did you do it? I looked up to you. You brought me into this shit." Mark's eyes began to water.

"Y'all lil niggas were coming up too fast, and before I knew it, y'all would've came past me, and I couldn't allow that," Ty explained. Mark didn't understand why Ty didn't want them to rise up in the game. The way they saw it, the more they made, the more Ty made because they never dealt with anyone else, but it was too late to wonder about that right now. The line had been crossed and there was no turning back. Just as Mark was about to pull the trigger, the front door came flying open, and Big Kev and D.J. came out licking off shots wildly. They didn't care who they hit, as long as somebody was put under their belt. Ty took off down the street as Mark dove behind a parked car. He lifted his MAC-11 over the hood of the car and began to shoot back. As quickly as the gun shots started, they ceased. When he peeped his head up, Mark saw Big Kev and D.J. laid out face down on the ground with Romeo and Lamont standing over them with barrels smoking.

"Go get 'em," Lamont shouted as Ty continued to run. Mark jumped to his feet and went after him. As he ran, all he had on his mind was revenge. Lamont and Romeo took off to get the car. Mark was only a few cars behind Ty when he stopped, took aim, and let off the entire clip. Ty's body did a summersault before slamming to the ground with a loud thud. Mark ran up on him and kicked him to turn him over to face him. Ty's body was twisted as he lay there. Mark relieved him of his gun and the knapsack.

"You got it all now, kid. Don't kill me!" Ty pleaded.

"This is for Alex and Lamont!" Mark told him with gritted teeth.

"Lamont?" Ty asked not remembering the name.

"Yeah, nigga. The brother of the girl you

gave that shit to."

Ty thought back to the girl and her little brother. He never thought nothing of the threat he received from the little kid five years ago after his sister took her own life with her daddy's gun, right after she told Lamont what Ty had done to her. To make matters even worse, she was eight weeks pregnant. If Ty would've known that it would cost him his life in the long run, he would've killed Lamont back then.

"See you in hell, nigga," Ty shouted, then closed his eyes tightly. Mark let off two gunshots into his head and throat. Mark ran his pockets and found a half-empty bottle of pills. After reading the label, Mark shook his head from side to side. Being that he was a straight-A student in health, he immediately recognized the AIDS pills. "So, these are what Ty was poppin' all of those times when he was around me," he thought as he reflected back to the many times he saw Ty take the pills. Mark thought he was poppin' some Viagra or something. Mark shook his head and headed back to the car, when a police cruiser slid to a halt and two officers jumped out with their guns aimed at him. "Drop the weapon and put your hands up," the officers yelled in unison. At that moment Mark's life began to flash before his eyes. The clothes, the jewelry, the money, the fame, the cars, Alex, Karen, him missing being an uncle, maybe even a father, Tosha and their last conversation— "Don't say good-bye, good-byes are forever. I'll see you later" —her beautiful smile. He couldn't leave her. "I was almost out," he said to himself. He wished he would've listened to his brother and let the shit ride, but now it was too late. He snapped out of his thoughts by the officer's warning again. He looked up and saw Lamont and Romeo creeping past. "I love you Tosha," he whispered as he lifted up the gun in his hand preparing to go all the way out.

"You got three seconds to drop your weapon!" was all the officer got out before gunfire filled the air.

~ ~ ~

As soon as Lamont and Romeo entered the house, they went straight to the master bedroom to search for the stash. They knew they didn't have much time before the cops would show up, so they navigated through the house with a quickness. When they got to the first door on the right, Lamont held his hand up high. After hearing a male and female arguing back and forth, Lamont signaled for Romeo to follow his lead. "3, 2, 1," he counted, ready to barge through the door and lay the couple down.

BOOM!!

The sound of a loud gunshot made Lamont and Romeo take a step back and re-evaluates their original plan. "Fuck it," Romeo decided, then rushed up to the door and kicked it in. "What the fuck you doing in here?" he asked Nicole. Lamont rushed in a step behind and was frozen in place when he saw Nicole standing naked in the middle of the floor with a smoking gun in her hand.

"I-I-I," Nicole stuttered, trying to find the words to explain herself.

"Get your fuckin' clothes on and let's get out

of here!" Romeo demanded. As he helped Nicole gather her belongings and get dressed, Lamont searched under the bed. Coming up with a small shoebox filled with money, he tucked it under his arm and ran into the closet.

"I know this nigga had more than a few thousand in this bitch," Lamont thought out loud. It only took thirty seconds of rambling for him to come across an army duffel bag filled with money. "BINGO!" Lamont stuffed the shoe box inside of the bag and threw it over his shoulder. When he stepped out of the closet, Romeo and Nicole were on their way out the door. Lamont followed suit and watched Nicole's ass bounce with each step she took until they were out of the house.

Once outside, Nicole almost lost what little food she had in her stomach when she saw Big Kev and D.J. laid out on the front lawn. "Bitch-ass niggas," Romeo cursed as he walked by the two corpses. Nicole couldn't help but look back as Romeo pulled her up the street.

When they made it to the car, Lamont had to know the answer to the questions that he had been dying to ask since the moment he walked into the room with Nicole standing there naked. "Yo, who's the chick, big homie?"

"This is Nicole. Mark and Alex's little sister. My little cousin."

"Damn if anything is little about her," Lamont

thought to himself. It all started to make sense

to him now, but there was one more question

that he wanted to ask, and that was why she

was there at the house in the first place. That

would be a question he would ask at a later time,

but for now they had even bigger problems up

ahead.

"LOOK!" Nicole pointed. Lamont and Romeo

looked up and immediately checked their clips.

They had a feeling things were about to get ugly.

"Get behind the wheel, Nicole, and if we're

not back in two minutes, drive home!" Nicole

looked at Romeo like he was crazy. Even

though Rodney had let her drive his Cadillac a

few times before, she had never actually driven a car without anyone else in it with her. She closed her eyes and said a silent prayer that she wouldn't have to that night. When she opened them, Lamont and Romeo were both out of the car, squatting low and heading up behind the two officers that were bent down behind their squad cars. Nicole lowered the driver's-side window and listened.

"You have three seconds to drop your weapon!" the officer yelled right before Lamont and Romeo stood straight up and opened fire and filled their backs with bullet holes . . .

Text Good2Go at 31996 to receive new Release updates via text message.

To order books, please fill out the order form below:
To order films please go to www.good2gofilms.com

Name: __ _____
Address:_____
City: _____ State: _____ Zip Code: _____
Phone:_____
Email:_____
Method of Payment: Check   VISA   MASTERCARD
Credit Card#:_ _____
Name as it appears on card: _____
Signature: _____

Item Name	Price	Qty	Amount
48 Hours to Die – Silk White	$14.99		
A Hustler's Dream - Ernest Morris	$14.99		
A Hustler's Dream 2 - Ernest Morris	$14.99		
A Thug's Devotion – J. L. Rose and J. M. McMillon	$14.99		
All Eyes on Tommy Gunz – Warren Holloway	$14.99		
Black Reign – Ernest Morris	$14.99		
Bloody Mayhem Down South – Trayvon Jackson	$14.99		
Bloody Mayhem Down South 2 – Trayvon Jackson	$14.99		
Business Is Business – Silk White	$14.99		
Business Is Business 2 – Silk White	$14.99		
Business Is Business 3 – Silk White	$14.99		
Cash In Cash Out – Assa Raymond Baker	$14.99		
Cash In Cash Out 2 - Assa Raymond Baker	$14.99		
Childhood Sweethearts – Jacob Spears	$14.99		
Childhood Sweethearts 2 – Jacob Spears	$14.99		
Childhood Sweethearts 3 - Jacob Spears	$14.99		
Childhood Sweethearts 4 - Jacob Spears	$14.99		
Connected To The Plug – Dwan Marquis Williams	$14.99		
Connected To The Plug 2 – Dwan Marquis Williams	$14.99		
Connected To The Plug 3 – Dwan Williams	$14.99		
Deadly Reunion – Ernest Morris	$14.99		
Dream's Life – Assa Raymond Baker	$14.99		

Flipping Numbers – Ernest Morris	$14.99		
Flipping Numbers 2 – Ernest Morris	$14.99		
He Loves Me, He Loves You Not - Mychea	$14.99		
He Loves Me, He Loves You Not 2 - Mychea	$14.99		
He Loves Me, He Loves You Not 3 - Mychea	$14.99		
He Loves Me, He Loves You Not 4 – Mychea	$14.99		
He Loves Me, He Loves You Not 5 – Mychea	$14.99		
Kings of the Block – Dwan Willams	$14.99		
Kings of the Block 2 – Dwan Willams	$14.99		
Lord of My Land – Jay Morrison	$14.99		
Lost and Turned Out – Ernest Morris	$14.99		
Love Hates Violence – De'Wayne Maris	$14.99		
Married To Da Streets – Silk White	$14.99		
M.E.R.C. - Make Every Rep Count Health and Fitness	$14.99		
Money Make Me Cum – Ernest Morris	$14.99		
My Besties – Asia Hill	$14.99		
My Besties 2 – Asia Hill	$14.99		
My Besties 3 – Asia Hill	$14.99		
My Besties 4 – Asia Hill	$14.99		
My Boyfriend's Wife - Mychea	$14.99		
My Boyfriend's Wife 2 – Mychea	$14.99		
My Brothers Envy – J. L. Rose	$14.99		
My Brothers Envy 2 – J. L. Rose	$14.99		
Naughty Housewives – Ernest Morris	$14.99		
Naughty Housewives 2 – Ernest Morris	$14.99		
Naughty Housewives 3 – Ernest Morris	$14.99		
Naughty Housewives 4 – Ernest Morris	$14.99		
Never Be The Same – Silk White	$14.99		
Shades of Revenge – Assa Raymond Baker	$14.99		
Slumped – Jason Brent	$14.99		
Someone's Gonna Get It – Mychea	$14.99		

Stranded – Silk White	$14.99		
Supreme & Justice – Ernest Morris	$14.99		
Supreme & Justice 2 – Ernest Morris	$14.99		
Supreme & Justice 3 – Ernest Morris	$14.99		
Tears of a Hustler - Silk White	$14.99		
Tears of a Hustler 2 - Silk White	$14.99		
Tears of a Hustler 3 - Silk White	$14.99		
Tears of a Hustler 4- Silk White	$14.99		
Tears of a Hustler 5 – Silk White	$14.99		
Tears of a Hustler 6 – Silk White	$14.99		
The Last Love Letter – Warren Holloway	$14.99		
The Last Love Letter 2 – Warren Holloway	$14.99		
The Panty Ripper - Reality Way	$14.99		
The Panty Ripper 3 – Reality Way	$14.99		
The Solution – Jay Morrison	$14.99		
The Teflon Queen – Silk White	$14.99		
The Teflon Queen 2 – Silk White	$14.99		
The Teflon Queen 3 – Silk White	$14.99		
The Teflon Queen 4 – Silk White	$14.99		
The Teflon Queen 5 – Silk White	$14.99		
The Teflon Queen 6 - Silk White	$14.99		
The Vacation – Silk White	$14.99		
Tied To A Boss - J.L. Rose	$14.99		
Tied To A Boss 2 - J.L. Rose	$14.99		
Tied To A Boss 3 - J.L. Rose	$14.99		
Tied To A Boss 4 - J.L. Rose	$14.99		
Tied To A Boss 5 - J.L. Rose	$14.99		
Time Is Money - Silk White	$14.99		
Tomorrow's Not Promised – Robert Torres	$14.99		
Tomorrow's Not Promised 2 – Robert Torres	$14.99		
Two Mask One Heart – Jacob Spears and Trayvon Jackson	$14.99		

Two Mask One Heart 2 – Jacob Spears and Trayvon Jackson	$14.99		
Two Mask One Heart 3 – Jacob Spears and Trayvon Jackson	$14.99		
Wrong Place Wrong Time – Silk White	$14.99		
Young Goonz – Reality Way	$14.99		
Subtotal:			
Tax:			
Shipping (Free) U.S. Media Mail:			
Total:			

Make Checks Payable To:
Good2Go Publishing
7311 W Glass Lane,
Laveen, AZ 85339